ROCK STARRED

KAREN BOOTH

ROCK STARRED

Copyright © 2015 by Karen Booth Balcom

All rights reserved.

No part of this book may be reproduced in any form or by any electronic or mechanical means, including information storage and retrieval systems, without written permission from the author, except for the use of brief quotations in a book review.

This is a work of fiction. Names, characters, places, and incidents either are the product of the author's imagination or are used fictitiously, and any resemblance to actual persons, living or dead, business establishments, events or locales is purely coincidental.

Cover image licensed from Deposit Photos.

 Created with Vellum

I SHOULD'VE COMPLAINED a second time to the building superintendent about the busted air conditioning. Really, I should have. But eighty-plus degrees? The rock stars were glistening so perfectly—especially Peter Barrett. It was a once-in-a-lifetime set-up for a photo shoot and I wasn't about to let it go to waste.

"Guys, I know it's hot, but let's get a few more shots before we take a break and try a different set-up." I crouched below eye-level of the four members of Slump. Late afternoon sun filtered through the lead-paned windows of my warehouse photo studio. If I could've bottled the beauty of that light, especially as it graced the stunning male specimens standing before me, I would have.

"It's freaking April in New York. It's not supposed to be so fucking hot. We're sorta dying here, Katie." Elliott, the singer, blew a fringe of sandy-blonde bangs from his forehead.

"Grow up," Peter chimed in. "Let her do her job."

"Just our luck with this freaky heat wave." I smiled and kept taking pictures. I photographed countless bands every year, and the ways in which they fought like siblings never failed to amuse me. Perhaps it was the product of being an only child. "The light is just so amazing right now." I held my breath when Peter unleashed a particularly penetrating stare. He was hot enough to make me drop my camera. And not just literally. "It'll be gone in a minute and there's no getting back good light."

I snapped the camera shutter like crazy. Sweat rolled down my back. My tank top clung to me. The hair I'd piled on top of my head in an effort to cool off threatened to topple. I kept moving though—side-to-side, up-and-down, capturing the four band members from every angle.

As instructed, the guys followed me with their eyes. I wanted them to confront the camera. I wanted raw intensity. It was a perfect match for the grinding, guitar-driven sound of the band *Rolling Stone* had just dubbed, "Kings of the Universe".

It might've made me a bit self-conscious to be firmly planted beneath their unflinching stares, although I always used the camera as a bit of a shield, but it was obvious that most of them had something else on their minds. Elliott, the singer, had been arguing with someone over his phone whenever we took a break. By the sound of it, I would've guessed he was in the midst of a break-up with a girlfriend, or he was at least trying to cut a woman loose. Mark, the bass player, was reportedly getting over a cold and very much seemed stuck in an antihistamine-induced haze. I sensed that the drummer, Tony—or as his bandmates called him, Stony—was in a different kind of haze, but he enjoyed having his picture taken and was a willing participant.

And then there was Peter—he wasn't merely following orders by keeping his eyes glued to me. Something else was going on. I felt it from five feet away. His brilliant blue was unusually intent, zeroed-in. Maybe he was just like that. Maybe he was fascinated by photography.

I hit the shutter a final time and rested the camera on my chin. "Let's take twenty. I'll see if we can find another fan and

I'll call the building manager and find out when the air conditioning is supposed to be fixed."

All four guys broke free from each other, heading in opposite directions, Peter straight for me.

"How's everything looking?" he asked.

So that that was it—he was worried about looking good in the photos. "I got some amazing stuff. You four are extremely photogenic. I promise that putting up with the heat will be worth it." I stepped over to the cameras and lenses littering the beat-up factory table I used for meetings.

Peter followed. "Photogenic? Have you looked at Elliot? He's ugly as sin. If we look good, I'm sure it's all your doing." He ran his hands through his messy and slightly damp, chocolate brown hair.

"That's nice of you to say. I'll try my best to get it right."

He cleared his throat. "You know, uh, I have to say that your work is really amazing. I don't want this to sound weird, but I've been a fan for a while now."

"Of me? You like looking at photos of other bands?"

Peter laughed and leaned back on the edge of the table. His stance made his slim-fitting black tee hitch up. The sliver of stomach above the waistband of his jeans was a little too distracting. "No. Your other work. The photos you take around New York. Your work in black-and-white, especially the urban stills, are pretty amazing."

This was a first. No band member I'd photographed had ever taken note of my other work. Those photos were about scratching my creative itch, it was the stuff for galleries, and only when I was lucky enough to find one to take me. "Where did you see my other photographs?"

"At a showing in LA. About six months ago. I bought one of the ones you took from under the Brooklyn Bridge."

"Really? Those are some of my favorites."

"It's in my place in Chicago." He held both hands out before him, splaying his fingers. "I hung it right above my bed."

I swallowed hard. Every new word out of his mouth held another humbling surprise. "Well, thank you. That's so flattering. I really appreciate it."

"Maybe we could go out for dinner tonight. You know, talk about your work, my work. Other things. Whatever comes up." He dropped his head to the side to ask for an answer. The flicker of electricity that came from his eyes suggested far more than sharing a meal.

Dammit. I filed through the reasons I shouldn't say "yes", but none of them felt particularly compelling when confronted with Peter. He wasn't just pushing my lady buttons. He was pushing my photographer buttons, too.

But I had to be strong. Dinner with Peter would just mess me up. It didn't take much for me to get attached, especially to a guy as smart and smoking hot as him. "I'm sorry. I don't think it's a good idea." It physically hurt to say it.

"Boyfriend?"

My stomach sank at the mere mention of the word. "Nope."

"I don't see a ring."

Coping with "boyfriend" was a breeze compared to the way "ring" made me feel. No, he definitely did not see a shiny platinum band with a 1.2 carat, ideal-cut diamond on my finger. Absolutely not. It no longer resided on my finger because I'd sold it and bought camera equipment to donate to a local high school. I'd considered throwing it in the East River, but in the end, I figured some good had to come from my misery.

"Nope. No ring either."

He smiled wide. "Perfect. You're unattached."

Unattached. That was such a simple way of looking at it. If only I was at a point where I could think of myself as one of two things—single or taken. "Peter, you seem like a great guy. I just try not to mix business and pleasure. Gets messy." I scrunched up my nose. My stupid excuse stunk.

"It's just dinner, and technically, if we go after you're done taking our picture, won't you be done with business for the day? We could forget work and focus on pleasure."

Why did everything have to sound so damn enticing coming out of his mouth? "Maybe the next time you come to New York." *That might buy me a few months. Maybe I'll be ready by then.*

"If you're trying to blow me off, you should know I'm an incredibly persistent man."

I shook my head. "You can have your pick of women. Hell, there are about fifty hanging out in the alley behind my building waiting for you guys to finish up. Don't expend a bunch of energy on my account."

"Funny, but I don't tend to find smart, creative, interesting women in alleys. I've tried, but it just never works out."

He had an answer for everything. That one even made me laugh. I'd had my fair share of come-ons from guys in his line of work, but none of them had come prepared the way he had, nor had any of them seemed so sincere. "I appreciate your effort to be outside the rock star mold."

He shrugged. "I'd rather spend time with a woman who's both beautiful and has a creative mind. I find that combination pretty damn hard to pass up. I'm curious to find out what makes you tick." He traced his finger in a circle on the tabletop. "Or purr, as the case may be."

For a good thirty seconds, I completely forgot how to breathe. Good God, I wanted to know what purring for Peter would be like. It'd been way too long since someone had made me feel like that.

It only got worse when I gazed into his puppy dog eyes. If only I could just tell him the reason why I kept guys in two categories—friends and the one-nighters, and that there was no being a member of both groups. Nothing ruined a friendship faster than sex. So where did that leave Peter? After all, he was saying everything I wanted to hear, precisely the reason to keep him where he was—a friend. Nice guys deserved better.

I picked up my phone. "Give me your number. We'll stay in touch. Maybe I'll come see you guys play some time."

He fished his own out of his back pocket. "That would be great."

As soon as I finished entering Peter's info, I had a text from my best friend, Gwen.

Ice cream.

I clamped my eyes shut. Talk about horrible timing. *Ice cream* was what Gwen and I had devised as shorthand for, "this is really fucking important so drop whatever you're doing and call me right now". Gwen generally used it when she had a fight with her boyfriend, Ted. I'd used it countless times during the events that eventually led to me selling my engagement ring.

"I'll be over in a few minutes so we can finish the shoot," I said. "I just need to make a quick phone call."

Peter nodded. "Of course." His voice was decidedly less enthusiastic now. I was probably insane for turning down a dinner date with him.

"Hey, honey. What's up?" I whispered, jamming a finger in my other ear and wandering off to a corner of the studio.

"Hey, so I didn't want to have to tell you this over the phone, but I start my shift at the hospital in less than an hour. There's no time for me to come over and tell you in person."

"Tell me what? Did somebody die?" My stomach sank with unease.

"Brad got married."

I heard the words, but they didn't add up. Not yet. Brad. Got. Married?

"To, you know. Her," Gwen continued.

Every step I'd taken to distance myself from what happened with Brad was erased with a sentence from my best friend. Suddenly it felt like I was face-to-face with my nightmare all over again. "Married. To her." I choked on that last word, fighting images of him in a tux, the girl he'd cheated on me with in a wedding dress. I was supposed to be the girl in the wedding dress. I was supposed to have the happily ever after.

"Katie, if you need me now, I'll see if I can get somebody to cover for me. We'll talk about it and drink beer and eat ice cream."

"No. No. I'm okay." I glanced across the room. Peter smiled at me. For some reason, that only made me want to cry more. But there was no time for tears and work always distracted me from the bad things. "I'm actually in the middle of a photo shoot right now."

"Okay, good. Go take pictures. I know it helps."

"It does. It helps a lot."

"You're stronger than this. Remember that."

I nodded, sucking in a deep breath. Was I stronger than this? At that moment, I wasn't sure I was strong enough to make it through the next five minutes.

But I had to get past this point in time, just like I'd gotten through every other miserable moment since Brad left that fucking note on the kitchen counter. I had to get through it because there was no other way. I just needed to keep myself on the path that had helped me through it, the path where I kept men at arms' length and focused on work. "I got it. I'm good. I promise."

"Okay, well, whatever you do, don't go on Facebook. You're still friends with his sister, right? She posted a zillion pictures."

"Yeah, I'm still friends with his sister. It's not her fault she has an asshole for a brother."

CHAPTER TWO

One month later.

WE BOTH SPOKE ENGLISH, but not much in the way of communication was taking place. The cabdriver grinned and nodded into the rear view mirror each time I insisted that he wasn't hearing me correctly.

"Sir. Please. The Mandarin. Man-da-rin." The air in the taxi was unbelievably stuffy. I gathered my hair, twisting it behind my shoulder.

"Yes. No problem," he said in a thick, Eastern European accent. "Mondrian."

"Am I hearing him wrong? Or is he going to take us to fucking South Beach?" I asked Gwen.

"Not sure," she said. She would never force the issue, even if someone were driving her twenty minutes and twenty bucks out of her way.

"Sir," I said, my voice growing hoarse. I scooted forward on the seat. "We are not going to the Mondrian. Please don't take us to South Beach. We're staying at the Mandarin."

"The Mandarin *Oriental*," Gwen added.

"Oh," the cabbie said. "Mandarin Oriental. No problem."

I exhaled and slumped back against the seat. "Thank God. Thank you."

"No problem," Gwen said and slapped my leg.

Fifteen minutes later, we arrived at the Mandarin—sleek, modern and ultra-luxurious. The doorman, unbearably handsome with dark hair, darker eyes and golden-caramel skin, greeted us with a blazing smile and more than a hint of flirtation in his voice. "Ladies."

Gwen snickered and shied away as we sauntered through the door.

"One last cocktail?" I nodded toward the bustling hotel bar. My buzz from the wine at dinner had fizzled and my inability to sleep well in a hotel prompted my need for a nightcap.

"Um..." The hesitation in her eyes was plain. She rarely stayed up past ten—too tired from her job at the hospital or exhausted from another argument with her live-in boyfriend, Ted. They were still on shaky ground after the last fight, which was the point of our getaway weekend. Gwen needed a break.

"How often do you get to dress like this?" I asked. She looked incredible, closer to twenty than twenty-eight, in a black silk top with beading at the plunging neckline and a pair of jeans that showed off her butt. Her coppery-brown hair rolled past her shoulders in waves. "You look way too hot to go to bed. Come on. Don't be a wimp. There's no going to bed early on girls' weekend."

The bar was packed, dozens of men in suits—gray, navy and more gray—a room full of tipsy businessmen.

Gwen came to a halt and grabbed my arm. "I don't know if I'm up to this," she said above the din of voices. "I was hoping we could just talk."

An attractive guy with sandy-blond hair and an expensive

suit sat at the bar. He slyly grinned at me and took a sip of his drink while he raised his eyebrow.

"It's just one drink. And I think I can convince somebody to buy them for us." Not that I needed anybody to buy me an over-priced martini. This was merely for fun. As far as I was concerned, there was no point in escaping to Miami for girls' weekend if we weren't going to do at least one thing that was completely out-of character.

I strode through the throng of men, swishing my blonde locks over my shoulder, hoping Gwen would follow my lead as she trailed behind me. It was not my usual approach. I eased into the spot behind him at the bar, resting my elbows and flagging the bartender. "Two mojitos, please."

Mr. Expensive Suit turned on cue and spoke to the bartender while looking at me. "Put them on my tab." He stared as if it were a form of seduction.

I looked him in the eye, unafraid but curious why he'd chosen the creepiest approach imaginable.

"Actually, these ladies are with me. I'll get their drinks." A deep, velvety voice sounded behind me.

A smile rolled across my face. *Whoa. A bidding war? This might keep Gwen's mind off things.*

I turned to a sight so out of context that my brain noticeably sputtered—Peter. My breath caught as our eyes connected and he unleashed his familiar, devilish smile.

I straightened, making a conscious effort to play it cool. "Peter."

He grasped my hand, holding on for a few extra heartbeats, sending a tantalizing shiver through me. "Katie, hi. This is a surprise. You in town for our show?"

"Your show?" I'd forgotten how wonderfully imposing Peter's tall, broad frame could be. I'd spent a lot of my life being "the tall one". I loved the way I felt petite next to him.

"We're playing tomorrow night." His gray t-shirt clung to his shoulders. I would've clung, too, if I was a t-shirt. His hair was its usual, well-arranged mess. He was a complete one-eighty from every other man in the bar, in the best possible way. He turned to the hulking figure approaching behind him. "You remember Tony."

The Slump drummer nodded and pushed his sunglasses up on to his forehead. "You're that photographer chick," he mumbled, pointing.

Peter grimaced and smacked Tony in the chest with the back of his hand. "Where are your fucking manners?"

Mr. Expensive Suit gruffly cleared his throat and grabbed my elbow. "I thought I was buying you a drink, gorgeous."

Before I could answer, Peter grasped my hand. "Sorry, guy. She's with me." He led me to the other end of the bar while Tony and Gwen tagged behind us. "What a loser." His lips might have been delivering words, but they were carrying on an entirely separate conversation with me. "He tries to buy you a drink and he thinks he can grab your arm like that?"

I raised an eyebrow and glanced at Peter's hand, still wrapped around mine. "Some guys will do that."

Gwen cleared her throat and parked her hand on her hip.

"I'm sorry," I said, shaking off the spell that Peter had cast on me. "Peter, Tony, this is my best friend Gwen. We're here for a girls' getaway."

Gwen smiled wide. Apparently running into a few rock stars was enough to improve her mood. "Hi. I love your band."

That was all the invitation Tony needed. "Gwen, is it?" He took her hand and blatantly peered into her cleavage. He towered above her, swaying, closing his eyes as if he might nod off at any moment.

I leaned and whispered in her ear. "They call him Stony."

Tony wasn't quite the stunning specimen that Peter was, but

he was attractive in a primitive, muscle-bound way. His beefy arms strained against the sleeves of his t-shirt and his head was shaved bald, which I already knew was one of Gwen's big turn-ons.

The bartender brought our drinks and Peter leaned into me as he picked up the glasses. "Katie." His steely blue eyes suggested several indecent acts in a tiny amount of time. "Why don't the four of us take this outside?"

Peter was dangerous territory. I'd known that the day I'd photographed the band. He was way too handsome, way too nice, way too willing to discuss photography, a topic I'd gladly go on about all day. Plus, I didn't have to guess with him. He'd made it clear he was interested, persistent with phone calls, emails and text messages over the last month.

We'd flirted during those exchanges. Big time. Things escalated, edging toward naughtier, more suggestive quips. Maybe I shouldn't have done it, but I'd wanted to. It was fun to have a back-and-forth with a witty and dead-sexy guy. More importantly, it was safe. Distance meant there was no risk of things getting physical, little chance of me getting overly attached. That led to hurt if I truly liked a guy and I couldn't help but like Peter.

He opened the door that led out to the terrace overlooking the pool. I attempted to go first but he pulled me aside and Gwen and Stony went ahead. Gwen turned to me as she walked, shrugging.

"I'll be out in a sec," I said.

Peter let the glass door close and gripped my elbow. "Katie, I have to say that I'm really excited that we ran into each other. Talk about luck." His thumb rubbed back and forth across my skin, his voice softened and became husky. "I hope you're happy to see me too. Your last text said you would think about it. That was a week ago and I've heard nothing since then."

He was just close enough that his smell was disorienting, a heady waft of musky man. "Sorry. I've been really busy. I had a photo shoot in England last week. Travel. Jet lag." The stuff about being busy was absolutely the truth, but it wasn't everything. The other piece of the puzzle was what exactly I'd said I would think about—an invitation to fly out for a weekend to see his band. It had sent familiar panic through me and all I could do was put my head down and get back to work. Work was safe.

"Okay." He glanced down at his feet and when he looked back up, his eyes were hypnotic, as if they were shiny pools of molten metal. "It's just that I like to know where I stand. I don't want to make an idiot of myself, you know, if I don't have a chance. Sometimes I have a very hard time reading you."

I tried to imagine a scenario in which Peter wouldn't have a chance with a woman. That seemed impossible. It was no surprise he had a hard time reading me, I was torn between a crushing dose of attraction and my rules of no attachments and no sleeping with guys I might want to keep as a friend. It wasn't fair to him, but that was already Strike One against Peter.

"We talked about this the day we met. I don't get involved with clients."

"Ah, but I'm not really a client anymore. It's been a month since you photographed the band."

"True."

"So? My chances? Because I'll leave you alone if you want me to."

Of course I didn't want him to leave me alone. I was dumb, but I wasn't stupid. "Why don't we just have a drink and see where that gets us?" Even that much felt as though I'd stepped too close to the fire.

"Talk about a non-answer."

"Surely you must appreciate the challenge of the unknown."

He laughed and shook his head. The soft light in the bar made his blue eyes blaze. It was enough to make me forget my name. "I love a challenge. When there's a payoff."

"Regardless of what happens, I'm sure you'll sleep like a baby tonight." I patted his arm, my breath hitching at how firm it was.

His eyes narrowed. "You're really just going to leave me flapping in the breeze, aren't you?"

"Sorry. No promises." I opened the door and glanced over my shoulder. Apparently the fit of my jeans was doing the job as Peter seemed to have difficulty closing his mouth. "Shall we?"

The thick, late-May Miami air filled my lungs in the darkness, a sliver of a moon the only light out on the terrace. Stony and Gwen were seated at a table at the far end, but we were otherwise alone. Stony's arm draped over Gwen's shoulders and I was dismayed to see that she wasn't objecting. Her boyfriend Ted was a good guy and although they argued a fair amount, they were perfect for each other.

"She has a serious boyfriend," I grumbled as we approached.

Peter snaked his arm around my waist and tugged me closer. He leaned down to mutter into my hair. "I'm sure she can take care of herself." The tip of his nose grazed my ear, the most innocuous brush of skin against skin, and yet it made me desperate for air.

We each took our chair and Peter scooted his right next to mine.

"So, girls' weekend. What does that entail? Picking up strange men and dancing on the bar?" Peter asked.

"Oh yeah," I quipped. "Body shots. Orgies. You name it."

"Sounds suitably hedonistic for the life of a beautiful rock photographer." Peter reached under the table and smoothed his hand over my thigh.

I took a sip of my mojito to cool the heat he'd just created between my legs. Every time he touched me my defenses dropped. "Actually, it's just an excuse to order expensive wine at dinner and sleep in."

"That sounds even better." Peter trailed his fingers north at an achingly slow pace.

Words were my only way to stay on equal footing, to counteract the ways he broke down my resolve with his hands. "That's one way to start things," I said quietly.

He slid his hand back down to my knee. "I'll start this any way you want." He cocked his head to the side. The look in his eyes became impossibly welcoming. He was up for anything and everything. No question about that.

"Good to know," I mumbled, bristling with curiosity at the gentle swell of his lips. What would it be like to kiss him? Sweet and soft? Fast and furious? Part of me was dying to know. The other part, the part that spends way too much time thinking, delivered a surprisingly helpful reminder—Peter could have any woman he wanted. Worrying that he'd want anything more than one night was worse than presumptuous, it was idiotic. He was in a band, on to the next town and the next girl after tonight.

So maybe this could work. Maybe I could give in to what I wanted and not leave Peter wondering any more. We could have our one night. If I were honest, it was perfect—it was all he was asking for, and all I was prepared to give.

Gwen smiled and her eyes flashed when Stony whispered in her ear. "Did you say something, Katie?" she asked with a giggle before she chugged the rest of her drink.

I cleared my throat and sat back in my chair, swirling ice cubes with the straw and glancing over at Peter, who cocked his eyebrow before winking at me. He absolutely knew that I was putty in his hands. "No. Nothing."

Stony leaned closer to Gwen. "Another drink, babe?"

"That would be great. These are so yummy. I think I could drink them all night."

Several mojitos later, things with Gwen had spiraled downward. She switched seats, deciding that Stony's lap was preferable to the cushioned patio chair. She wiggled as she laughed and I assumed there was no way for Stony to stand up without his jeans telling us how much he was enjoying her company.

"They like each other," Peter whispered with hot breath against the sensitive skin beneath my ear. He'd snuck his hand into the back of my slinky top moments earlier. I couldn't help but smile when he made a sound akin to "Eureka!" as he realized I wasn't wearing a bra. "Like us, right? Tell me you like me, Katie." He slowly slid his way around my rib cage, his surprisingly soft hand cupping the underside of my breast and his fingertips grazing my nipple.

The languid pace of his caresses was like honey dripping from a spoon, so intoxicating that I closed my eyes, feeling as if I might lose control. "I do like you, Peter. You're cute." My head dropped closer to his as if he was the metal and I was the magnet.

"I've had better reviews."

"Sorry. That was just the first thing that came to mind."

Gwen turned her back to us, sharing a quiet moment with Stony. I studied her body language and cursed the day he was brought into the world. In an instant, she suggested we adjourn upstairs for a continuation of the evening's festivities. I glared at her and excused the two of us to the ladies room. Peter wore a content grin as we got up from the table and Stony swayed again.

"Gwen, honey, you do realize what's happening here, don't you?" I asked once we were alone in the bathroom. "Because if you go upstairs with Stony, I assure you that you're not going to be playing Tiddly Winks."

She stared into the bathroom mirror with a glazed expression, her mascara smudged under one eye. "Do you have any idea how long it's been since Ted looked at me the way stoner Tony is looking at me?" She fixed her mascara, her pale-green eyes twinkling from the mirror. "And you know what? I deserve to have a guy look at me like that. Tony is fun and he wants me, Katie. You would not believe the stuff he said to me. Dirty stuff." She opened her eyes wide as if she was trying to sober up. "What's up with you and Peter? Jesus, he's hot."

I set my purse on the vanity. "Yes, he is, and you know me, one step at a time."

She smiled in the mirror. "Yeah, right. You and I are both getting lucky tonight."

My mouth gaped. "Whoa. Okay. We need to talk. You are *not* sleeping with Tony. Give me two secs."

I took a three-mojito pee, grumbling to myself about how crazy Gwen was acting. "Gwen, honey, this is a really bad idea," I called out to her. She didn't respond and I tucked in my blouse. "Gwen? Hello?" I zipped up my pants and stepped out of the stall to an empty ladies' room lounge. "Fuck."

CHAPTER THREE

PETER and I tracked down Stony next to a potted palm by the elevator, but Gwen was nowhere in sight. I called her phone and got voicemail, but I had a text from her as soon as I ended the call.

Second thoughts. Tell Stony I'm sick. Have fun.

I breathed a sigh of relief and replied. *Got it.*

I shook my head in mock dismay. "Oh damn. Sorry, Tony. It sounds as though Gwen is sick. Probably too many mojitos."

Confusion washed over his face. "Sick, as in I'm not going to see her again tonight?"

"Too bad, huh? Sorry." My lower lip jutted out. Hopefully, no one would notice I was going for the Oscar with this performance.

"You could always head downtown, man. See some bands or something," Peter said. He pushed the up button on the elevator.

"Okay," Tony said, with a hint of defeat in his voice. "I'll ask the doorman where I should go to find women. Catch you guys later."

I took solace in watching Tony walk away. Crisis averted.

Peter slid his hand to my lower back, gently pressing my hips into his. "Finally we're alone." He dipped his head and softly brushed his lips against mine.

I was about to surrender to the kiss when the ding of the elevator kept us from violating any rules of public decency. "Yes, alone."

We stepped into the dimly lit elevator. As the door slid closed, Peter took my hand and gently looped my hair behind my ear. He allowed his lips to skim the dip between my shoulder and neck. I steadied my hand on the metal handrail as his mouth and tongue sent need shuddering through me. Each subtle, craving movement of his lips was another reminder of how badly I wanted him.

We got out on the eleventh floor and Peter keyed his way into his room at the end of the hall. I heard the door close as I stepped into the beautifully appointed suite, the king bed with the golden silk duvet already turned down for the night.

Peter came up behind me and wrapped both arms around my waist. He gently kissed my neck and muttered, "I'm a good guy, Katie, I swear."

My chest heaved as I sucked in a breath. *That's what worries me.* "I know you are."

"It's hot in here," he said.

I turned and my breath caught in my throat as I watched him lift his t-shirt over his head. His chest was incredible—firm and muscular but not overbuilt. An enticing trail of dark hair ran down his flat stomach below his bellybutton, leading my mind below the waistband of his jeans, low-slung around his hips. My cheeks flushed. My entire body felt as though someone had cranked the thermostat.

"What's your poison?" he asked as he bent down and opened the minibar.

I kicked off my heels and smoothed my hands over the landscape of his back. "I don't need a drink."

"Mmm." He twisted around and wrapped me up in his arms, kissing me tenderly. His tongue slid past my lips, playfully encouraging mine to tangle with his.

My hands slid along the contours of his trim waist, my fingers stopping when I felt the inviting curve of his hipbone. I reached down and cupped the rock-hard ridge in the front of his pants. He kissed me, moaning into my mouth when I pressed into him with the heel of my hand. I unzipped his jeans and let them drop to the floor.

He circled his hands over my lower back and nuzzled my neck with balmy, sweltering breath. "Will you do something for me?"

"Maybe," I answered with a rasp in my voice.

"I want to watch you take off your clothes. Slowly."

I pushed down on his shoulders and he sat perched on the edge of the bed. I stood inches away from him. If I was going to get the most of my one night with Peter and he wanted me to do all of the work, it was going to be on my terms. The anticipation of the evening ahead was too lovely not to savor. "Okay," I said. "I'll take off my clothes for you, but no touching."

He leaned back on his hands, his cock stiffly standing at attention inside his black boxer briefs. His legs were lanky but solid, with a raised scar across one of his knees. "What's the point if I don't get to touch you?"

"You do eventually. Think of it as a game. We can see how much self-control you have."

"I can already tell you it's almost zero. Especially when I'm around a beautiful woman and I have a raging hard-on."

I smirked at him. "Humor me." I began slowly, my fingertips tracing the neckline of my top. I pitied him as his gaze traveled up and down my body and he seemed to wrestle with a few impulses. I crossed my arms and gathered the hem in my hands. Peter's eyes flashed with anticipation as I showed him a sliver of my stomach. I turned away and slipped my top over my head. It skimmed my back as it dropped to the floor. The bed creaked. Heated breaths grazed the small of my back. "No cheating." I glanced over my shoulder to find his hands hovering near my hips.

I cupped my breasts, rolling my head to the side and quietly moaning as even my own hands felt incredible against my skin. My nipples puckered and grew taut as I turned back to him.

"Move your hands," he said.

"Like this?" I asked, biting my lower lip and rolling them in circles, my breasts full and firm.

"No." He closed his eyes for an instant. "I mean, yes. That's hot, but I want to see you."

I fought a smile and peeled back my fingers, watching his Adam's apple bob when he swallowed. His eyelashes were absurdly long and dark, his lips beckoning. Glancing down, I wondered how long his cock could stand to be contained. I eased closer and reminded him, "No touching. Not yet." I moved my breast close to his mouth, his hot breath huffing against my skin. I lowered my chin to my chest as he eyed my nipple and the anticipation engulfed me. "You can use your tongue, but no hands."

His lower lip sat just beneath the tight bud and he flashed his eyes up at me before taking my breast into his mouth. My eyelids drifted shut as the tip of his tongue teased me with deft swoops, delicate circles and pleasing flicks. I longed to stretch out on the bed and relinquish control, have him take command, but that would have meant abandoning my game, and this particular game left me in charge. As much as it was physically painful to do it, I pulled away from him.

I smoothed my hands over my stomach and unbuttoned my

black pants. Peter grinned as I undid the zipper and the fabric slid down my legs. I turned away again and used my thumbs to wriggle my lacy boy shorts down my hips. I looked back over my shoulder to see him eying my ass as if he hadn't eaten in days.

"How are we doing back there?" I asked.

"You're fucking driving me insane. Let me touch you." His lips inched closer to my lower back and I felt weak in the knees.

I smirked. His frustration was insanely cute. "All in good time. Lie down." I turned as he did what I'd asked. "Scoot back on the bed. Put your head on the pillow."

He watched me while crawling backward on his elbows. Without question, he was one of the best-looking guys I'd ever been with, if not the best. His features were angular, his nose had an adorable bend to it, and I wondered if he'd been a jock when he was in school. He certainly had the body for it. Not as if he'd been a football player, but long and lean, as if he'd played baseball or run track.

He sat up. "Jesus, Katie. Just get over here. Now."

"Relax. I want you to lie back down and close your eyes."

"You aren't one of those freaky chicks who's going to tie me up or steal my clothes, are you?"

I arched my eyebrows and planted my hands on my hips. He closed his eyes but I could tell that he was trying to peek as a mischievous smile played at the corners of his lips. "No look-ing." I knelt on the bed and he wrapped his hand around my leg. "You have a very hard time following rules, don't you?" I trailed a finger down the center of his chest along the tempting path of dark hair that led to his bellybutton and then beyond, beneath the waistband of his boxer briefs. "Do you want me to keep going?"

He smiled. "What do you think?"

I peeled back his boxers and his thick erection sprang free. As soon as I touched him, his silky skin pulsed and I relished how iron-hard he was. "Mmm," I said and took him in my mouth. I sucked softly, riding his muscular length from base to tip, pausing to tease the ultra-sensitive ridge of the head with my tongue.

He moaned and arched his back. "You should jump in at some point or I'm going to finish before you even get started."

I straddled him. "I find it hard to believe you can't keep it together." I spread my hands across the patch of hair in the center of his chest. "You can touch me now."

I fully expected him to act like a kid and go crazy on me. Peter, however, merely opened his eyes and placed his hands behind his head. "So you want me to touch you. Really? I thought you were just going to do everything yourself."

"Very funny. Now's your chance to be in charge, big guy."

"What if I just lie here?"

"What if I just leave?"

"You wouldn't do that. You're as worked up as I am."

"You're so fucking sure of yourself, aren't you? I find that highly annoying."

"Most women love it." He reached up with one hand and grazed my nipple with the tip of his finger. He smiled at me, wholly satisfied with himself. "Come here." His strong hands gripped my hips and urged me closer.

I leaned forward and placed my hands on either side of his head, my hair cascading down around us. "Tell me you have a condom," I mumbled, burying my face in his neck. Impatience prickled my spine, the shadow of stubble along his strong jaw bristled against my cheek.

"In my wallet. Jeans pocket."

I hopped up from the bed as if I was a runner after the starting shot, but caught myself and tried to play it cool. My little foreplay tease had revved me up way more than I would call normal, or maybe it was that Peter had me so turned-on that everything between my legs was calling the shots. I handed him his wallet and he slid out the foil pouch, presenting it to me in his open palm. "Would you like to do the honors?"

I bit my lower lip as I knelt next to him on the bed. "Gladly." I opened the packet and opted to start by licking away the bead of moisture that had collected at his tip. He groaned and squirmed. Our eyes connected as I rolled on the condom. He seemed to take great delight in watching.

"Are we going to do this?" I asked and straddled him.

"Yes, we are." He pressed his hands firmly into my lower back, just enough pressure for his cock to rest against my folds and amplify my already teeming frustration. He sucked my breast into his mouth, starting a staggering cycle of tongue and teeth, pleasure following torment and back again.

My body responded with a slick pool of heat between my legs. I rolled my hips and slid along his length. His tip caressed my clit with every backward stroke.

He grinned and rolled to his side while tugging on my arm. I stretched out, wriggling back and forth against the smooth and silky sheets. He spread my legs with his hands, long, strong fingers clutching the tender skin of my inner thighs. Greedily, he leaned down to kiss my lower stomach a dozen times before separating my swollen folds with his fingertips.

He pressed his lips against the warmth, his tongue circling my clit, every rotation inching me closer to my peak. I clamped my eyes shut and knocked my head back as he slipped a finger inside, my hips bucking as he curled it masterfully into the bundle of supersensitive nerves. It was as though he had a road map to my entire body, managing to home in on the very thing that I most wanted at that moment.

Peter bracketed my hips with his hands and hovered above me, dipping his head to kiss my mouth with moist lips. I locked my ankles under his ass, urging him inside as the ache between my legs blazed. He toyed with me, building anticipation as his cock grazed my center before he took a long, fluid thrust. I gasped and my body gave in, molding around him.

We rocked together in perfect pitch, my hips lifting off the bed as he ground against my pelvic bone. He groaned and I smiled on the inside, sensing the tension in his body was already close to the bursting point. I arched my back, wanting him even closer. Electricity bubbled under my skin. It rolled through my belly, building steadily behind an invisible barrier until the current broke through in a barrage of pulses.

My body hungrily pulled on his and Peter braced his forehead against mine, driving himself deeper and with greater force. My fingers dug into his lower back, taken by surprise as a second wave began to crest in me while I was still reeling from the first. It came quickly, my body overly sensitized to his motions, his weight and his seductive smell. He became rigid as a board and I heard his breath catch in his throat. He grunted and keened forward as he throbbed inside me, thrusting with a careful rhythm. I sucked in a breath as a second orgasm tumbled out of me, circling waves of pleasure, more intense and fiery than the first.

Peter collapsed on top of me, both of us struggling for breath. He rolled to my side and swept his hair from his forehead, damp with sweat. "Damn," he said. "I actually think I like the no-touching rule." He placed his palm on the side of my face and kissed me tenderly. His hand sat on my stomach and he did nothing but look at me for moments, his nose inches from mine.

I couldn't help but wonder what he was thinking, if he was going to tell me I should think about going soon.

"Katie, you're so beautiful. You knock the wind right out of me." He leaned down and ringed the end of his nose around my bellybutton before kissing it, making me giggle, something I almost never do around a man. "You know, I wanted you from the minute I laid eyes on you. I couldn't stop watching you the day of the photo shoot."

A disconcerting rush of emotion fluttered in my stomach. "You're sweet, but I'm already naked and in your bed. You don't need to worry about sweet-talking me."

He furrowed his brow. "Most women like it if I say that their shoes are cute. I'm not feeding you a line."

"Oh." My chest thumped in an unfamiliar pattern. "I'm sorry. I just, well, never mind..."

"There's no way I'm the first guy that's told you that you're beautiful and sexy and amazing." He kissed my stomach again with his mouth open, tracing his tongue in a tiny circle against my skin. "Men must tell you that all the time."

"No. You're not the first." He just happened to be the first who sounded as if he didn't expect anything in return.

CHAPTER FOUR

"HAS the sun always been this bright?" Gwen asked with disdain. "Whose idea was it to come to Miami, anyway? It's so sunny here."

We sluggishly ventured to the shadier side of the pool deck where there were several open chaises. Men and women reading the likes of *The New York Times* and *Vogue* bathed in the sunniest spots, apparently unconcerned with premature aging.

Despite the inviting beauty of the crystal-clear infinity-edge pool, there was no one in the water and the day was already showing signs of becoming a scorcher. Midmorning and it had to be in the upper eighties.

The pool boy in white tennis shorts and polo rushed over to spread terry covers on our chairs and I wondered why any grown man would take a job where he was referred to as a boy. Maybe it was the implied sex benefits, that every woman's fantasy was a romp in the towel room with the pool boy.

"I'm Julian. I'll be your server today, ladies. May I start you off with a mojito?"

My stomach lurched at the thought of mint, rum and lime.

Gwen groaned and buried her forehead in her hand while she slumped down into her chair.

"Thanks, Julian. I'm thinking iced tea for us this morning." I set my pool bag next to my chair. "You doing okay over there?" I asked Gwen, patting her on the knee.

"Uhh. Do you have to be so loud?"

I smiled and shook my head. "Sorry, honey. I'll try to keep it to a dull roar."

I reclined, draping my forearm across my face. The sun was just high enough in the sky that it blanketed my legs in warmth. I slid my cover-up to the top of my thighs and sank further into the chair while I tried to convince myself that I wasn't hungover like Gwen, I was merely taking my sweet time.

Just as my stomach chose to do a few somersaults, someone loudly cleared his throat. I lifted my arm and peeked through one eye.

"Morning. Feeling a little rough?" Peter was breathtaking, damn him, shirtless in long black board shorts and Ray-Bans, unfortunately accompanied by Stony.

The only discussion Gwen and I'd had that morning was when she made it clear she wanted to stay as far away from Tony as possible.

"I'm good. You?" I asked, perplexed that he was seeking me out the morning after. Maybe he was the rare guy who bothered making the effort involved with friendship after sex, an arrangement that never really worked.

"I feel great. May I?" Peter gestured to the chair next to mine but didn't wait for me to answer before he dropped his towel and a paperback and stretched out. "I missed you this morning." He dragged his fingertip along the top of my hand. "Why didn't you wake me before you left?"

I pulled my hand into my lap. "Do you have to announce it?" I sat upright and propped up the back of my chair.

He leaned closer and pushed his sunglasses up onto his forehead, his eyes sparkling more brilliantly than the pool. "Oh Katie. Come on," he whispered. "You're not a prude. You proved that last night." His eyebrow arched in a playful, but cocky way.

I glanced over Peter's shoulder at Stony, who was standing at the foot of the empty chaise next to Peter, looking confused. Gwen had turned away from us, likely hoping that her flirtation with Stony had been a bad dream. A gray-haired man was asleep on the chair next to hers, leaving Stony to fend for himself.

Peter followed my line of sight and glanced over his shoulder. "Tony. Sit. We're staying. Unless you want to go find the rest of the guys."

"Staying?" I asked as Stony plopped into the chair.

"I like the view. Is that okay? Next round is on me."

"I'm drinking iced tea. They give you refills."

"Fine. I'll buy you lunch."

I watched him, his eyes sweeping across my face and narrowing. It was different seeing him in the light of day, knowing I wasn't going to sleep with him again. The air held a tinge of sadness. We'd already had our fun together and we'd had so much fun I was surprised I could walk without a limp.

"Okay," I said. "Lunch could be okay."

An attempt at friendship we would make—surely no harm in hanging out and having lunch. He was fun to be around when he wasn't being arrogant, even though just looking at him made me squirm in my own skin.

Peter settled in with his book and Stony slid a baseball hat over his face. I tried to relax, taking a stab at reading a magazine. Unfortunately, sitting next to Peter was driving me berserk, the temptation to look at him too great. He made me lose my place when his finger wandered to my chair and grazed my thigh. I took a deep breath, attempting to ignore the brush of his skin.

This was precisely why it was so difficult to be friends with a guy after sex—the attraction was still there, only now I knew how good it felt when we gave into it.

I stood and tossed my hat onto the chair before lifting my cover-up over my head. I'd taken only a single step when I heard his voice.

"Hey, Katie. Want some company?" Again he didn't wait for the answer but folded the corner of his page and hopped up from his chair. He smoothed his palm over the bare skin of my hip. "You look amazing." He eyed me, I'd like to say it was from head to toe, but he seemed to be concentrating on the middle-most parts. "I'm serious." He took a few more steps and dove in, making the tiniest splash imaginable.

I strode to the wide steps into the pool. With one toe in, it became obvious why Peter and I were the only ones taking a dip. The water was nearly the same temperature as the air, like a lukewarm cup of coffee, not the refreshment I'd hoped for. I waded until I was in to my waist in the shallow end.

Peter was doing handstands in the deep end, his long feet wagging. He could stay up for a good ten seconds before he'd flip over and come back up for air. I swam to the side, folded my arms on the hot concrete and set my chin on my hands. My legs floated near the surface and I closed my eyes, enjoying the gentle lap of the waves Peter was creating from the other end.

There was a splashing sound and I soon felt droplets of water on my back. Peter was next to me, swiping his wet hair from his forehead, his brilliant white smile tugging at me as I placed my feet on the pool bottom again. "So what's the plan tonight? Stony and I have sound check at four, but we don't go on until ten. Do you and Gwen want to grab dinner?" He moved closer and trailed his fingers down my spine. "Or we could ditch those two and have dinner alone." His eyebrows shifted up and down.

I had a fuzzy recollection of the reason Slump was in town—their sold-out show at one of the big rock clubs downtown. "Right. You guys are playing tonight. Gwen and I should probably go out on our own for dinner. It's the only night left of our girls' weekend."

He held his hand to his brow and scanned my face. "Are you not okay with what happened last night? Because I thought it was spectacular." He moved his hand to the tender underside of my arm, caressing my skin beneath the water.

I didn't know what to say and he put me off track every time he touched me. "It was great, but we should probably just stick to lunch. I don't want to make things any more complicated than they have to be. For me or for you."

"What exactly is so complicated about dinner?"

"Nothing, but you and I both know we're talking about more than dinner."

"Of course we are. I have all sorts of tricks up my sleeve. Although I won't be wearing sleeves."

I had to smile at his goofiness, even when he was frustrating the hell out of me. "I'm sure your tricks would blow my mind, but I don't do more than one night. And I assumed that you were on the same page. I mean, you're in a band. Isn't that your thing? I just assumed that one night was all you wanted, too."

"Hey. Don't make assumptions. It's not cool." His eyebrows drew even tighter in confusion. "We had an amazing night together and we get along great. Why is dinner and another night together a big deal?"

"It's a big deal to me. A really big deal." I wasn't about to launch into the story behind my rule while I was chest-deep in water with dozens of strangers within earshot. One night had been tested. I knew my limits. I knew the places my heart was all too eager to go.

He grumbled and shook his head. "I have to say this is a first.

And I have to admit that I admire you for having the balls to do what guys do all of the time." He reached into the water and scooped a handful over the top of his head, sweeping his hair back. "But I'm not other guys. I think you should break your rule for me." He reached for my hand, his eyes a pale and icy blue in the blazing midday sun.

"Give me one good reason."

"This." He slid his other hand around the back of my neck, threading his fingers through my hair. His mouth against mine was soft and wet. He pulled back only a few inches and I could feel his breath on my lips. "Seriously, what do I have to do to convince you to give me one more night?"

I gnawed on my lower lip. My brain felt as if it had been turned upside-down. With shimmery beads of water along his shoulders and collarbone, he was irresistible. The question only made the situation more disorienting. No man had ever asked me such a thing. The few who stuck around long enough for the explanation always seemed to take it at face value, willing to walk away and move on. "I don't know."

"You want to spend time with Gwen? Have dinner with her and spend the night with me." He took my hand and raised it to his perfect lips, kissing the back of it lightly. "The whole night."

My stomach knotted at the thought of breaking the rule that had protected me so well. A second night would mean one thing, I was only going to get more drawn in to Peter. How could I not? I needed time to process this. "Can I think about it?"

"Of course you can." His thumb rode back and forth over my knuckles. "But I think you already know the answer. I think you want to and you just don't want to say it."

CHAPTER FIVE

"YOUR TURN," I announced to Gwen, wrapping my hair up in a towel after my post-swim shower. I stepped out of the bathroom to see her perched on the edge of the bed, looking deep in thought. "You okay?"

She frowned. "I called Ted. I feel guilty."

"You didn't tell him, did you?" I plopped down next to her and she popped up on the mattress. I wrapped my arm around her. "It was just some flirting. You had the sense to stop before you did anything stupid."

"What was I thinking in the first place?"

I bit my tongue. I'd been wondering the same thing. "You were drunk and he's sorta cute."

She responded to my answer with a quizzical look.

"There's the rock star thing," I said. "Every woman has that fantasy, doesn't she?"

"Apparently you do. Is Peter number four or five?" She picked at her fingernail. "Not that I blame you. He's ridiculously hot."

"I don't exactly keep track, but it's more like two. Maybe three."

"Well, whatever the number is, clearly you're not rock starred out yet."

"One could argue that it's an occupational hazard."

"Even though those are exactly the kind of guys who don't stick around?"

Fuck. Gwen had missed her calling as a talk-show host or a therapist—her talent for getting to the heart of the matter was unmatched. That was precisely what I'd done. The handful of one-nighters I'd had since Brad had all been that type...guys who don't stick around. Even though he'd said he was different, there was a good chance I'd just found another one in Peter. I played it off with a wave of my hand. "We weren't talking about me anyway."

"Why is that?" She turned and crossed her arms across her chest, her eyes accusatory. "When we hang out at home, we only talk about me. You know things about my relationship with Ted that nobody else knows, but I know nothing about what's up with you anymore."

"That's not true. I tell you about work." I bent forward and unwrapped my hair from the towel, flipping it back and letting it roll over my shoulders. "There is no relationship stuff in my life. You know that."

She shook her head slowly. "That world is your own creation. Nobody is forcing you to have your rules."

The corners of my mouth drew downward. Apparently the only person in my life who understood my rules no longer considered them useful.

"Look," she said. "I get why you did it. Brad hurt you. He treated you like shit. But it's been more than two years and you need to try a different approach." She planted her hand on my knee. "You didn't used to be like this, hooking up with guys like they don't mean anything."

I pursed my lips. My shoulders tightened. "I don't treat guys like they're nothing. I just don't get involved. There's a difference."

She groaned. "That's not you. That's some alien version of Katie you invented. You can't do this forever. You have to open up to someone or you're going to end up alone."

I crossed my legs and looked up at the ceiling, avoiding eye contact. The agony of what had happened two years before washed over me like high tide, muted only slightly by time. I'd grown a thicker skin, learned to protect myself since then. Even so, it didn't take much to conjure the memory of coming home from my final wedding dress fitting to Brad's note, the one that would change my life forever.

A giddy thrill had worked its way through me when I saw Brad's familiar handwriting scrawled on a piece of paper on the kitchen counter. I was sure it was another love note. He used to leave those for me all the time. We were so close to our big day. I couldn't have contained my excitement if I'd wanted to.

Instead, I got a string of injurious words scrawled on the back of an envelope about how he wasn't sure he'd ever really loved me, there was somebody else. He had to leave, be true to his own heart, before it was too late. He wanted me to know that it was better for both of us. Every word left a hole in me, some of them bigger than others, and I'd been trying like hell to close them since.

How could I have been so unequivocally wrong about someone? Questions like that still haunted me. "Maybe I'm still not ready."

"The longer you keep doing this, the more it's going to seem normal. And it's not normal." Her lovely green eyes held a familiar mix of pity and love. "You're like a sister to me. I can't watch you do this to yourself anymore. You need to learn to keep the past where it belongs and give some guy, somewhere, a chance."

"I want to. I'm just scared." My voice dragged as I battled the tears and overwhelming sadness that came when I thought about Brad.

"You have every right to feel that way, but you have to let down your guard at some point."

The room went silent as my mind swirled with bad memories, like I was swimming my way out of a whirlpool. Maybe I could put it behind me. I blew out a breath through my nose, my shoulders dropping in defeat. "I suppose you're right."

Gwen knocked her head to the side and wriggled her finger in her ear. "What was that?"

I huffed. "You're right."

Her eyes opened wide in disbelief. "Let me find a tape recorder. You never tell me I'm right about anything."

"That's because it's annoying to admit."

She smiled wide before pulling me into a hug and patting me on the back. "Okay. Tonight. You and I are going to go have a fabulous dinner and drink wine so you can tell me what Peter looks like naked."

I crinkled my lips and swallowed.

"Then we're going to get in separate cabs," she said. "I'm going to come back here and order crème brûlée from room service and take a bath in our insane bathtub. You're going to go see Slump and you're going to relax and have fun and just be Katie. Let life happen."

"You aren't coming with me?"

"No way. I don't ever want to see Stony's face again."

"What do you mean let life happen?"

"I mean you need to just go with something. Give Peter a chance."

CHAPTER SIX

I CLIMBED out of the cab in front of Club Moxie, first astounded and then discouraged by the line of people two or three across, down the sidewalk and around the corner. It felt as though it was a sign. I was ready to bail when I saw that there was a separate window for will-call tickets with only a few people waiting.

I stepped up to the glass after the guy in front of me collected his tickets and leaned to speak into the hole. "Kate Stillman. I'm on the Slump guest list."

A woman with black spiky hair dragged her finger down a long list of names and flipped to a second page. I could see my name scribbled down at the very end. "Do you have a plus one?" she asked.

"No, it's just me."

She crossed my name off the list. "Hold on two secs. I'm supposed to let security know that you're here." She mumbled into a walkie-talkie and then leaned forward to talk to me through the glass again. "It'll be a minute. They'll come and get you."

I stepped away and wrapped my arms around my middle,

wishing I'd had the sense to throw on a cardigan or jacket before we'd left the hotel. It had rained during dinner and it felt as if the temperature had dropped a good ten degrees, making my silky, sleeveless top seem like seemed an idiotic choice, no matter how good I felt about the way I looked in it.

Gwen had given me endless amounts of encouragement throughout dinner. Her words were all well intended, but they didn't bolster my confidence at all. They only made me question what I was doing. A second date seemed like a suicide mission, my heart and pride hanging in the balance. For all I knew, Peter just wanted a farewell fuck before he hit the road with the band the next day.

The line to get into the club dwindled and I wondered if I'd been forgotten. *I should have just gone back to the hotel with Gwen.* I didn't want to be a princess, but waiting alone on a dark sidewalk wasn't exactly the VIP treatment I was accustomed to. I dug my phone out of my purse and was about to send Peter a text when a metal door scraped open and a burly guy in a too-small t-shirt leaned out. "Are you Katie?"

"Yep."

"Come on. This way."

He led me down a dingy hall, covered with band names scrawled in pen and marker. We rounded the corner and he stepped aside when we reached a wood door, which he pushed open for me.

The band's dressing room was packed with people, almost all of them women, a few looking as though they'd answered a casting call for jailbait. At the ripe old age of twenty-eight, I wondered if I was already a relic, an annoying concept considering that Peter had only recently turned thirty.

Every band member had a girl or two hanging on him except for Peter, who sat in the corner with his back to me, strumming his guitar and poring over a notebook. Lead singer Elliot gave me a look of confused recognition as he stood opening a beer.

Stony caught my eye as a big-chested blonde fingered his bald head. "Yo, Pete," he called out. "Your *chica* is here."

Peter looked over his shoulder, his brilliant blue eyes and electric smile flashing when he saw me, causing my heart to worm its way into my throat. He hopped up and set the guitar against the wall, stepping over a few groupies to get to me, stopping to slug Stony in the arm and give him the stink-eye along the way.

"I was starting to worry." He put his arm around me and kissed me softly on the corner of my mouth. "Let's get out of here." Taking my hand, he led me into the dingy corridor where a few crewmembers and club employees milled about. He leaned me against the wall in a dark corner and gave me a steamy beer-flavored kiss, his fingers twining with mine. "I'm really glad you decided to come." He swept my hair behind my ear. "You look so beautiful in that top. I wish we had time to run out to the bus for some alone time."

As much as it was my natural instinct to dig in my heels, his words left me unable to keep my hands to myself, my fingers drawn to the patch of his chest peeking out from his black, collared shirt. "Doesn't that mess with your mojo?"

He grinned and looked at my hand as my finger swirled in his chest hair. "You're thinking of athletes. It actually does the opposite for musicians." He kissed me again, prompting the now regular flutter in my chest. "So Gwen decided not to come?"

"She wants to stay away from Stony."

"Probably for the best. He's hooking up with some girl who's been hanging around all day. You know how it is."

I did know how it was. I'd freaking lived how it was. The thought of Peter acting like that was wholly unpleasant, even when I knew that he must do it all the time. There was no shortage of available women.

"I should go find a spot out in the club to watch the set." I hitched my purse over my shoulder.

"Oh no. You don't have to do that. You can stand on the side of the stage with the rest of the girls."

I crinkled my lips. *The rest of the girls.* "Great."

Peter escorted me to the side of the stage where three other women stood, clustered behind the curtains that were already open. He pecked me on the temple. "Time to make the donuts," he said and walked back to where his band mates were waiting.

The girls were all talking, oblivious to me. I checked my phone for messages just to have something to do when I overheard them.

"I hooked up with him the last time they were in town," the tall redhead said. "Guess that's not happening this time."

Stony's blonde clucked her tongue. "Elliot is hot and he's the singer. Some people might say that's a step up."

"Yeah, I guess," the redhead answered.

My pulse began to thump wildly as I did the math and realized unless she was talking about Mark, the very married bass player, she had to be talking about Peter. That left me with an uneasy roll in my stomach.

The club was packed, a throng of sweaty and anxious music fans. It was a much smaller venue than Slump would normally play. They were building buzz for a live record that would come out in the fall by selling out every show in record time.

You could sense the anticipation in the air as the music over the PA changed to an instrumental version of Slump's most recent hit, *Clouded.* The crowd pressed closer to the stage as people craned their necks in hopes of being one of the first to see the band. Stony led the procession, taking his seat behind the drum kit and thumping the bass drum a few times. The crowd erupted a roar of screams and cheers, which only grew louder when Elliot and Peter took the stage.

The audience became more eager, chanting the band's name. Peter looked down at his feet, tuning his guitar. He stomped on an effects pedal, cocked an eyebrow at me and strode to the center of the stage with more charisma than I ever imagined could be crammed inside a body. I watched as he sent an entire mob of people into a state of euphoria with a single strum of his guitar.

By the middle of the first song, I'd nearly forgotten where I was. I became immersed in the performance, astounded by how tight they were as a unit. Their musicianship far surpassed anything I'd imagined. It was obvious that the magic on the record was entirely their own, effortlessly replicated in a live setting. Watching Peter was more than a little bit of a turn-on, seeing him masterfully play guitar, arms glistening with sweat, his hair sweeping across his forehead. Girls screaming for him from the first few rows, he peeled out several mind-blowing solos. He was in his element, with a visceral rock swagger all his own.

He sauntered over to me after the set as the band stood in the wings, waiting for the crowd to earn their encore. "Let's get out of here right after these last two songs."

I smiled, eying his sweat-coated chest and forehead, his hair slightly damp from the moisture. "Don't you want to hang out with the guys afterward?"

He leaned into my ear with hot lips against my skin. "Not when I can be alone with you."

———

SITTING in the back of the limo with Peter, it felt as if we were stuck in bumper-to-bumper traffic, except I was fairly certain we'd hit nothing but green lights. We couldn't keep our hands off each other. He kissed me a few times, but each instance quickly became incendiary, hands slipping under clothing, fingers grasping, tongues winding together. We would stop, sit back and collect ourselves, smoothing garments and catching our breath. Then one of us would break down and look at the other and we'd both give in to temptation again.

Peter flattened me against the wall of the elevator on our way up to his room. "I think I played better tonight because of you. That was the best show I've had in a few weeks." He firmly gripped my rib cage, his thumb grazing the side of my breast. "You're wearing a bra. That's no fun."

My eyes fluttered. Even fully clothed, every brush of our bodies stoked the fire. "I have a feeling I won't be wearing one much longer."

The elevator dinged. "Yeah, not if I can help it."

We hurried down the hall at a lightning pace, holding hands. Peter jammed the keycard into the door and it flashed a red light. He tried a second time. Red light. He glanced up at the room number. "Shit. We got out on the wrong floor."

I snickered and grabbed his hand. "The stairs will be faster."

We walked double-time for the door at the end of the hall and took the steps up one more floor. The keycard flashed green this time and we stumbled into the room.

"Shower?" he asked, stealing a kiss as he slid his hand around my waist. "I'm sweaty."

I'd already started on his shirt with one more button to go. "Um, sure. Whatever you want." The thought of him wet and soapy was more than a little appealing.

"Anything? Will you loofah my back?" He rolled his shoulders from his sleeves, the expanse of his chest a welcome invitation.

I laughed quietly and kissed his shoulder, his skin salty and sticky, a sensory delight. "Are you serious?"

"No. I just like saying loofah." He grinned when I giggled, sweeping my hair to the side, exploring my neck with his velvety lips.

We stepped into the bathroom, leaving on only the light in the hallway, which cast a warm glow across the white marble floor. Peter reached into the glass enclosure and turned on the water. His jeans and boxers were gone in seconds as I tossed my blouse on the floor before wriggling out of my jeans.

He snaked his hands around my waist, his erection sandwiched between us. "I can't wait to cover you in soap." He didn't hesitate to unhook my bra and pop each strap off my shoulder. "Much better."

My breasts flooded with warmth before he even touched them. It was such an unfamiliar feeling—that Peter and I already had a tiny sliver of history and I wasn't panicking, I only wanted his hands all over every inch of me. He poked his thumbs beneath the waistband of my panties, pushed them past my hips and we stepped into the spray.

I sought his lips, resting my arms on his broad shoulders and combing my fingers into his now-damp hair. The hot water battered my back and trickled over my shoulders as the bathroom air became balmy and thick. His hands slicked down my back and over my butt, gently squeezing, drawing my hips closer to his. He sucked my lower lip into his mouth and our tongues swirled together in an endless loop.

Peter kissed his way along my jaw, down my neck and across my collarbone. He dipped his head to my breast and I watched his tongue circle the hardened tip of my nipple as water cascaded across the side of his face and rolled over his jaw. He held my rib cage firmly and dragged his tongue to the other breast, leaving a tingly trail in his wake. He took my nipple into his mouth as if he couldn't get enough of me. I dropped my head, grappling with how insanely good it felt.

I reached for the bar of soap and pressed it into his hand.

He unleashed a sly smile and snickered. "I didn't want to say anything, but your boobs are filthy."

"Very funny. You're the dirty one."

He built the lather with his fingers while the hunger in his eyes made me quiver. His sudsy hands sank against my breasts, his palms into my nipples, spreading the silky bubbles in circles. His eyes flickered as he watched my reaction, our eyes connecting while the temperature continued to climb. I gasped as he plucked at my puckered skin with his fingertips and began to gently twist, every turn sending a sizzle between my legs.

"You like that?" he asked, a satisfied smile across his face. He continued to roll my nipples between his fingers, building pressure in my belly.

"Yes," I whispered, struggling to force words from my body. The only instinct I had at that moment was to find a way to have him inside me as quickly as possible.

He slipped a hand between my legs and I popped up onto my tiptoes. "You're so wet," he mumbled and took a nibble of my ear as his fingers went to work.

"I want you so bad," I replied, surprising myself with the honesty of the admission. I reached for his rock-hard cock and he groaned as I stroked and curled the tips of my fingers under his balls. The heel of my hand worked against him as he backed me against the shower wall. As hot as it was in the room, the marble was icy against my back, causing me to arch into him.

He dropped to his knees and his hands separated my lips before he nestled his face between my legs. His tongue flickered against my clit as he drove two fingers inside, rougher than before. He grasped the back of my thigh with his other hand and hooked my leg over his shoulder. My head began to swim as this new position gave him the perfect angle to go even deeper and suck my skin voraciously, his lips hungry and eager. I steadied myself against the wall, clawing at the hard stone, knowing I might collapse like a rag doll when he was finished.

Pleasure coursed between my legs and my body clutched his fingers tightly, released, and grabbed again. The tension doubled within me as he pushed me higher and I begged him to keep going, gasping his name. I dug one of my hands into his wet hair and I grazed the tip of my nipple with the other. It felt as if every ounce of energy in my body was leaving my limbs, gathering in the center, until there was simply no more room. Peter used more pressure as he circled my clit with his tongue and that was enough to send me careening off the cliff into a joyous free fall, floating back to earth on a fluffy cloud of steam.

I lowered my leg as I caught my breath and he stood, kissing me with craving lips coated with my juices. I reached for his cock again, which was impossibly hard. "Your turn," I said, licking my lips, desperate to have him in my mouth.

My fingers dragged against the ripples of his back as I knelt on one knee and then the other. I grasped his muscular ass, licking my lips as I studied his impressive, steely length. The water pounded against his stomach, dark curls of hair dripping with moisture. I wrapped a hand around the base of his cock and lowered the tip to my mouth.

Pressing my lips together, I kissed the silky skin of his head. I circled my tongue around him gracefully, using a light touch as my lips clung to him, moving until I reached the supersensitive ridge. I took his head in my mouth, sucking while my tongue swept against his pulsing skin. I retreated to the tip, flicking my tongue at the slit before I enveloped his head again. His groan was enough approval for me to repeat the action dozens of times as I firmly pumped at the base with my hand. I looked up to see him drop his chin, eyes half closed.

I loosened my grip, claiming more of his length with my mouth. My lips rode along his thick and rigid cock, my cheeks suctioning. I caressed and cupped his balls with my fingertips while my thumb rubbed the bulging vein running along the underside. Peter dug his hands into my hair and gripped my scalp, his breaths growing shorter. He then reached down, grasping my upper arms and urging me back up to him.

I stood and he swept the twists of hair from his forehead before he brushed his lips along my jaw, his nose below my ear. "That was mind-blowing but I want to be inside you." He turned off the water. "Come here."

He clutched his hands beneath my butt and hoisted me up. I wrapped my legs around his waist and my arms around his shoulders as he maneuvered our slippery bodies through the bathroom and to the bed. He laid me down gently, stopping to kiss my chest and one of my breasts before he stole away for an instant, returning with a condom. He rolled it on while he watched me, his dark hair still dripping water into his face. Beads of water collected on his chest and in the tempting curves of his hipbones. Looking at the intensity in his face, I knew that any hesitation I'd had about sleeping with him a second time had been time and effort wasted.

He slid his hands beneath my hips, lifting them off the bed, pulling me closer as he remained standing, teasing me apart with the head of his cock, in total control. He claimed me with one long thrust, his eyes clamping shut as I locked my ankles around his waist. Everything about him was irresistible at that moment—the way he took charge, the way he turned me on all over again every time he touched me, the way he tended to my pleasure before his own. Even details like the fringe of his wonderfully long eyelashes made me want to stay.

He pumped slow but hard, cradling my ass with his hands and I braced for another wave. Pleasurable moans escaped his lips as he increased his pace. I could feel the boil coming from his groin, hear it in his voice as his breaths grew shorter and he muttered my name. I loved hearing him say "Katie", especially when it was coupled with words like "yes" and "more". His thumbs dug into my hipbone as he drew out every thrust and his full length rode in and out of me. I tried to hang on for as long as possible, but it was too much, and I called out several times before he pulsed inside me, dropping his head farther with every ripple of his release.

He set my hips on the bed and stepped away to the bathroom. I was so wonderfully spent that I couldn't do much more than close my eyes and smile. When he returned, he climbed onto the bed next to me and pulled me close. I settled my head against his shoulder.

"That was worth the torture of the limo," he mumbled, his lips pressed to my temple.

I laughed softly. If I could've melted into him, I would have. "Yes. Every minute."

"I should probably call the front desk and ask housekeeping to change the sheets," he said. "The bed is pretty wet."

"Maybe next time we should towel off a little after getting out of the shower."

"Sorry. I was feeling a little eager."

I curled closer to him and he traced his fingers over the contours of my hip. "Don't call housekeeping. They'll just ruin the moment. Plus, I have a hard time sleeping in a hotel anyway. I'll probably be up most of the night, wet sheets or not."

"Sounds like a challenge. Is that your way of saying you want me to wear you out some more?"

I smiled and smoothed my hand over his stomach, playing with his bellybutton. "I just can't sleep in a strange place. That's why I left last night."

"We're in a hotel. Your room is just as strange as mine. Is that really the reason?"

I suddenly found my voice caught in my throat. "It's not all of it."

"Do you want to tell me why you have your one-night rule?"

I propped myself up on my elbow and studied him. How had the feeling that I could trust him come so soon? Or was it just because his pull on me was so strong? "I was engaged once. He left me a week before our wedding for another woman."

He reached for my hand, which was still parked on his stomach. His eyes brimmed with concern. "I'm so sorry, Katie. No wonder." He turned onto his side to face me. "I had a really bad breakup once. I know it's hard to get over that sort of thing." He combed my hair behind my ear with his fingers. "Guys can be jerks."

I studied his face, getting lost in the beautiful parts of him and the way he'd laid his caring nature bare. I didn't share my past with most men, figuring they wouldn't care or even worse, they'd think there must be something wrong with me. After all, a guy who supposedly loved me had left me right before our wedding. Peter seemed to understand how badly I'd been hurt. Perhaps it was because he'd been hurt badly, too.

I sat up and pulled the duvet over us, settling in. "Don't worry," I said. "I'm not going anywhere tonight.

CHAPTER SEVEN

I WOKE to the smell of breakfast and Peter's tempting stubble-covered face, complete with a new feature—dark-rimmed, damn sexy, nerdy glasses.

"Wake up, sleepyhead," he said, caressing my arm.

I stretched and squinted as a sliver of sunlight beamed through a crack between the hotel room curtains. "What time is it?"

"Nine. I hope you're hungry. I ordered enough breakfast for a hockey team."

I sat up, clutching the duvet to my naked chest. "Nine o'clock? Seriously?"

"Yeah, I don't really believe your whole thing about not being able to sleep in a hotel room. You were out like a light last night." He stood at the edge of the bed, wearing only a baggy pair of pajama pants that hung low around his hips. He tugged on my hand. "Come on. Time to eat."

"I have to pee. Are my clothes still in the bathroom?"

"Here." He tossed me a gray t-shirt. "You can wear that."

I threaded my arms through the sleeves, noticing how

immodest the garment was when I stood. "Got anything longer?"

"For you? No." He glanced over his shoulder while making his way to the room service cart. "You look perfect as far as I'm concerned."

I shuffled into the bathroom, shocked that I'd been able to sleep so well. My hair was a kinky mess from going to bed with a wet head. I combed through it with my fingers, giving up when it only bounced back in disarray. I gathered my clothes from the floor and put on my panties.

Breakfast was set up on the table at the far end of his suite. We uncovered plates of waffles and sausage, bacon and eggs, potatoes, fruit and toast. He poured me a cup of coffee as I stared at the food, unsure where to start. There would definitely be leftovers.

"You're taking the breakfast is the most important meal of the day thing a bit far," I said.

"I couldn't bear to wake you up to ask what you wanted. You were so peaceful and you have a very sexy droop to your lower lip when you're sleeping."

"I do?" I rubbed my mouth with my hand, feeling my cheeks flush. "Oh well, thanks for all of this. It looks great."

He scooted his chair closer to mine and began heaping food onto his plate. "I'm starving anyway. I usually eat after the show." He shook a heavy dusting of black pepper on his eggs and dug in.

I helped myself to half of the waffle, adding strawberries. "I didn't know you wore glasses." I took a bite, crispy and golden on the outside, fluffy and soft within.

"I wear contacts. I can go put them in if the glasses are bothering you."

The contrast of his masculine rock star persona and dreamy bare chest with the geeky glasses was almost more than I could take. I considered asking if we could do it right then and there between the maple syrup and the marmalade. "No. I think you look cute."

He took a drink of orange juice. "I wasn't really going for cute."

"Sorry. Would sexy be better?"

"Better, but I'd venture to say incorrect."

I sipped my coffee, in awe of how at ease I felt with him. "Have you had glasses for a long time?"

"Since junior high. They didn't exactly make me a babe magnet."

"I'm sure you did better than most guys."

His cheeks turned an adorable shade of crimson. "I, uh, no..." He squinted and pinched the bridge of his nose. "Never mind."

"What? Tell me." I gently rubbed his forearm. "I'm dying of curiosity now."

He shook his head and smiled. "I didn't get my first girl-friend until I got contacts. That wasn't until after high school. I was nineteen."

"No way."

"Believe me, I would not make up such a pathetic story. It doesn't really help with the whole rock star image. I probably shouldn't have even told you."

I gathered my napkin in my lap and peered into his electric blue eyes. "Maybe you trust me."

"I suppose I do." Peter reached in front of me for the sausage, putting his arm around my shoulder and stopping to peck me on the temple. "What about you? I'm guessing you had the entire football team fighting each other in the school parking lot."

"Uh, no." I smiled wide and pointed to my teeth. "Not even close. Braces. Retainer. Headgear. I was an orthodontic nightmare." I dished bacon and eggs onto my plate. "I've made up for it since."

"I have no doubt about that."

Out of nowhere, a pang of uncertainty rolled over me. The morning after was normally my time to escape. I'd usually formulated my plan by now, but all I wanted to do was stay with Peter, even when everything was up in the air. With the hurdle of the second time sleeping together behind me, I still had no clue if he thought of this as the end. He would be continuing with his tour, me returning to New York and work. I only knew that I wasn't ready to be done, exactly the feeling I had feared most.

Someone even more pessimistic than me could argue that if this was the end, it was for the best. Peter's life was in Chicago. It would never work. And what would "work" even mean? Surely not a relationship, although a long distance one could be a good way for me to ease into it. The differing circumstances of our lives left me a little empty and sad.

"When do you have to leave?" he asked.

I hadn't eaten much, but the thought of our time together coming to an end had dampened my appetite. "A few hours. Our flight leaves at two."

He smoothed his hand across my thigh. "Any chance you can take a later flight? Next show is in Atlanta tomorrow night. The bus doesn't leave Miami until midnight tonight."

Dammit. What an offer. I would've paid a hundred-dollar re-ticketing charge for even five more minutes with him, but I had responsibilities waiting for me at home. "I wish I could. I have a big shoot on Tuesday that I need to prepare for and my neighbor is taking care of my cat. She doesn't like to do it for more than a few days."

He frowned. "Hmmm. Okay. That's too bad." He poured himself another cup of coffee and topped off mine as well.

"Well, we should make a plan for a week from Saturday then."

I blinked in rapid fire. "A week from Saturday?"

"We talked about it last night. Remember? The band is playing in New York?" His eyes narrowed, as he seemed to realize that I had no idea what he was talking about. "Huh. Maybe you'd already konked out at that point. You fell asleep on me, you know."

"I did?"

"You did. Maybe you can come to Philadelphia the night before. It's a quick train ride or I could send a car for you."

My brain reminded me that making plans was just another way to get attached, but my heart stepped in and insisted that everything would be okay, at least for a little while longer. Peter leaned closer, his heavenly face pulling me in and ushering away any remaining shred of nervous thought.

"I'll have to see about Philly and how that plays out with my work schedule," I said, "but I wouldn't miss the New York show for anything." I took his hand, weaving my fingers between his. "It sounds great." My heart thumped like a puppy wags its tail, happy for the attention.

"I hate the thought of being away from you for two whole weeks. We're just getting to know each other. I guess the phone will have to make up for it." He moved even closer and kissed me softly. "I really like you, Katie."

My heart now felt as if it was doing a tumbling routine. I welcomed the unavoidable smile on my face and inhaled his intoxicating morning smell. "I really like you, too."

———

MY NEIGHBOR, Mrs. Gunderson, gave me the full report on everything she and Max had done during my weekend away—

the number of times he'd hawked up a hairball, the number of times she'd entertained him with his favorite toy, the laser light.

"Katie, dear, I think he needs to have a different kind of food. He's getting a little pudgy."

"You think so? I don't know." I scooped up Max and he burrowed his furry head into my neck, purring so loudly that I almost couldn't hear myself think. "He looks like a handsome boy to me."

"Did you have a nice time on your trip?"

"I did." I watched as she widened her eyes, plainly asking for more details without a word. "I met a guy. I mean, I ran into a guy I know and we spent some time together. He's coming to the city a week from Saturday."

She nodded approvingly. "That's nice, dear. It would be good to see you settle down. I had three children by the time I was your age."

The start of the settle-down speech had a familiar ring to it, the same one I got from my mom at the 4th of July, Thanksgiving and Christmas. Neither she nor Mrs. G knew that I was proud of myself for sleeping with somebody two nights in a row and still speaking to him later. Given my recent history, that was up there with picking out a china pattern.

"Are we still on for our cookie-baking date on Saturday?" I asked. "I cleared my busy shoe shopping schedule for you."

"Only if you want to. I don't want to be a burden." Mrs. G took great joy in baking, something she'd often done with her daughter until she'd moved away.

"Don't be silly. I would never pass up chocolate chip cookies and the chance to catch up on the neighborhood gossip."

CHAPTER EIGHT

BEFORE HEADING TO MY STUDIO, I puttered around the apartment Monday morning with the last of the laundry and some bills when I heard the buzzer for the front door. I pressed the button on the intercom. "Yes?"

"Flowers for Katie Stillman."

I furrowed my brow. "Come on up," I said into the speaker, holding the button. I glanced down at Max, who was doing figure eights around my ankles. "What do you think, buddy? Somebody sent me flowers. When was the last time that happened?"

The hall echoed with the sounds of the delivery guy stomping up the stairs. He rounded the corner, a large spray of striking lavender roses disguising his face. "Wow," I said as he handed me the clipboard to sign and I took the vase. "Thank you."

I carried them inside and plucked the card from the plastic fork.

Katie,
Thanks for a perfect weekend. Can't wait to see you again.
Peter

I blew my bangs from my forehead. It didn't exactly work out with the last guy who'd given me flowers. Still, it was hard to escape the romanticism. Peter was pushing buttons again—buttons I didn't know I still had.

My phone sat on the bed. Peter deserved a call or at the very least a text, but my brain felt as if it were rolling around in my head. It was scary not knowing where this was going. When I was in control, with my rules in full effect, I always knew the destination even if it was going to be a very short trip. I sank down on the mattress and Max leapt onto the bed with me as I dialed Peter's number.

"Katie, hey," he said when he answered. "Whatever did I do to deserve a real phone call?" He asked the question with a distinct air of knowing exactly what I was about to say. "Not that I didn't enjoy our extended text exchange last night."

The smile prompted by his voice was inevitable. "You know what you did. Thank you for the flowers."

"They're beautiful. Such an unusual color."

"I thought they'd match the flecks of purple in your blue eyes."

My heart made a funny little pitter-pat. "I have flecks of purple in my eyes?"

"You do. I find them particularly mesmerizing."

I became so light-headed that I thought I might swoon. "Thank you. That's so sweet. I love them. You couldn't go wrong with the color, but I appreciate the extra effort."

"Good. I'm trying my hardest to keep from going wrong."

I heard giggles in the background, a woman's laugh. She sounded close, unpleasantly close, and it was only ten a.m. "What are you up to?" My pulse raced and I took a deep breath, stopping short of digging my fingernails into my thigh.

"I'm in the lobby of the hotel in Atlanta. Just waiting for our room keys."

"Who's there?" I was angry with myself the instant the question left my lips—flowers, a promise of a date when he came to New York. It didn't give me a claim on him, even when I was starting to feel as though I wanted one.

"Two secs," he said. There was a rustling on the line. "Hey. Sorry about that. I had to get away from Stony and the idiotic girl he met Saturday night. She followed us from Miami. She laughs at every fucking thing he says. Luckily we vetoed girl-friends on the bus."

"Oh. Sure." I blew out a breath quietly. *Stop worrying.*

There was another string of muffled sounds on his end of the line. "Katie, hey, sorry. I guess everybody's ready to go. Can I call you back in ten minutes?"

"I need to get to my studio and prepare for that shoot. I have a million emails to answer. Can we talk later?"

"Of course."

I chewed on my lower lip. "Tonight?"

"Yes. I'll call you before we play."

———

THE TIME I'd spent preparing for Tuesday's photo shoot, with a young, hot shit band called No Picnic, had been time squan-dered. The session started in a nightmarish fashion and slid downhill from there. After a hellish day of dealing with bratty rock stars, I left my studio in Tribeca to walk to my loft apart-ment in SoHo. I had so much annoyance and anger coursing through me that I wondered if I might summon the strength to stomp a hole through the sidewalk.

Normally I'd call and bitch at Gwen, but my only urge was to talk to Peter. I kneaded my forehead, a headache brewing. I just needed to get this out of my system and Peter was the perfect sounding board. He knew bands. I figured he could relate.

"Katie," he answered after the first ring. "This is a nice surprise."

"Oh, hey, thanks. How are you?" I kept up with my ultra-fast New Yorker walk, even though I wasn't in a rush. The summer heat rose from the asphalt, creating what felt like an oven.

"Are you okay? You sound stressed."

"Do you know the guys in No Picnic? They're that new band from Dallas that did all of the big festivals earlier in the summer."

"Oh, right. Talk about flavor of the month. Is that who you were shooting today?"

"Yes, it was a disaster."

"What happened?"

An annoyed grumble escaped my throat. "Sorry. I'm not mad at you, just letting off some steam."

"No. It's fine. Tell me everything."

"Are you sure?" I stopped at the corner and waited for the walk signal. "This is stupid. You know, I feel better just hearing your voice."

"Well, good. I'm glad that helps, but I still want to know what happened. And I love hearing dirt about other bands."

I smiled and crossed the street, continuing on my way. "They showed up two hours late and then they had the balls to tell me they were on a tight schedule."

"Amateurs."

"Oh, and you'll love this. The lead singer had about fifty pimples including a giant one right between his eyes."

He laughed. "Classic. It sucks being a kid. I'm guessing he spent a long time in makeup."

"You have no idea. It took forever. It was this huge ordeal.

The whole band kept complaining to me about the makeup artist and then I overheard one of the guys tell his manager that I was not only a bitch, but not that great of a photographer. They all basically scowled at me whenever we took a break in the shoot. Of course, they had no problem posing when I was taking their picture."

"What a bunch of punks. I can't believe they treated you like that. They'd better hope we never end up on the same show. I'd love to give them something to complain about."

I turned the corner on to my street with an embarrassing grin plastered to my face. The thought of Peter sticking up for me, of being protective, made everything brighter. "Are you offering to be my muscle?"

"Uh, yeah. You obviously need it. You are an insanely talented photographer. They're lucky you agreed to take the job in the first place."

I keyed my way into my building, still smiling from Peter's potent brand of macho sweetness. "You're so sweet, but I'm not *that* talented. I'm good. I won't say that I'm not good." After grabbing my mail, I continued up the stairs.

"Are you kidding? I put my foot down about hiring you. The rest of the band wanted that hotshot L.A. guy, Bruce what's-his-face."

"Bruce Flack? He's freaking amazing."

"He's no Katie Stillman."

My cheeks flushed. "You really are way too nice to me." There was a note from Mrs. G waiting on my door when I got to my apartment. "Hey, Peter, I should run. My neighbor accepted a delivery for me. I need to go get it."

"A delivery, huh?" he asked in an oddly quizzical voice. "Keep me on the line. I want to talk more about the photo shoot."

"I didn't know you were behind the band hiring me." I

stuffed my mail into my bag and started down the stairs to Mrs. G's unit.

"Full disclosure, I'd also seen a picture of you, but you know that wasn't the only reason I wanted to hire you. I swear."

I knocked at Mrs. G's door. "We'll have to talk about that later. Hold on the line for a minute." I tucked my phone into a mesh pocket on the front flap of my messenger bag.

"Katie," she chirped when she answered. "You won't believe the flowers that came for you today."

I twisted my lips. "That's weird. I got flowers yesterday. Maybe they delivered them twice by accident."

She padded back into her apartment as I stood in the doorway, surveying the fussy perfection of her unit, resplendent with pristine fifties furniture and a china cabinet full of vintage cookie jars. Mrs. G. shuffled toward me with another vase of lavender roses. "These are just lovely. They're such a unique color. Are they from the young man you met in Miami?"

I blushed, wondering if Peter could hear. *Young man.* Mrs. G made it sound as if he was courting me. "Maybe. He sent me flowers yesterday," I said softly. I took the card and opened it before she handed me the arrangement.

Dear Katie,

Yesterday's romantic gesture didn't seem like enough. Miss you.

Peter

I tapped the card against my chin as heat again flooded my cheeks.

"Well?" she asked.

"Yes. They're from him," I said loudly, for Peter's benefit. "What a goof."

She smiled and placed her hand on my forearm. "I'd say he's a keeper."

Flowers in tow, I returned to my apartment and set them on

the flea market coffee table in the living room, next to the previous day's arrangement. I fished my phone from the pouch and plopped down on my modern gray sofa.

"I'm back."

"So I'm a young man, a keeper *and* a goof. Good to know."

Now I was certain my face was several shades of crimson. "Thank you for the flowers. Again. It's so nice of you. You really didn't have to do that."

"Katie, come on. Doesn't a guy get any bonus points for being extra romantic?"

I cradled the phone between my ear and shoulder and settled back on the couch, my headache and miserable day a distant memory. "You get all kinds of bonus points. It's up to you to decide how to use them."

CHAPTER NINE

THE REST of my workweek was a blur—scouting locations, sending proofs to clients and booking my travel. I was exhausted by the time I stumbled home each night, although the arrival of another dozen roses every day improved my mood considerably.

The flowers always came with a different note.

Wednesday's said he wished we were in Miami again, together.

Thursday's said that all he wanted was to see was the flecks of purple in my eyes.

Friday's flowers carried a request for me to help him with his mojo. I deliberated about picking up the phone as I changed into workout clothes. I'd had to fight the urge to call him all day because my schedule had been so packed. I was eager to say "thank you", but I also knew I'd blow off my thirty minutes on the treadmill if I didn't get it over with.

My water bottle went in the cupholder, and my phone on the magazine rack. Ten minutes into my run, I had a text from Peter.

Whatcha doing?

I grinned and slowed to a jog. *Running.*

And texting? Dangerous.

Talk later?

Run later?

I smiled, pushed the red "stop" button on the treadmill and hopped off. Sitting on the wide plank hardwood floor with my legs splayed, I leaned against the sofa. Max looked up at me and went back to sleep. I was still catching my breath when my phone rang.

"So, which is it? Texting accident or did you decide to give up on fitness for today?" Peter asked.

"You're so impatient."

"I'm bored."

"I thought you spent all your time on the phone with the florist. Thank you for today's flowers. I love them just as much as I loved the others."

"You're welcome. I can't help myself. It's habit now."

I blinked several times, still thrown off-kilter by every sweet thing he did for me. "Only a week until we get to see each other." I shook my head at the seductive tone of my voice.

"Only a week? The anticipation is killing me. Please tell me we get to have a sleepover at your place."

I laughed. "Is that what we're calling it?"

"Do you have another suggestion?"

"Pajama party?"

"There will be no pajamas."

"Excellent point." I glanced at the clock. It was only a few minutes after six. "When do you guys go on tonight?"

"Not until ten. I'm just sitting in the hotel room by myself. The rest of the band went to dinner."

"Aren't you hungry?"

"Nah. I'd rather talk to you."

Max jumped down from the couch and stretched, waving

his orange-and-white-striped fluffy tail and rubbing against my leg.

"What do you want to talk about?" I asked.

Peter cleared his throat. "What are you wearing?"

"What?" My cheeks warmed.

"Tell me what you're wearing right now. Tell me everything."

"I just got off the treadmill. I'm wearing black workout pants and a tank top."

"Katie, come on." He groaned adorably. "Work with me here. I miss you. You gotta sell it. Are you sweaty?"

A peculiar mix of embarrassment and fascination crept over me. Phone sex? Could I do phone sex? "Oh. Okay. I'm sorry." I walked across the apartment to my bed, kicked off my shoes and took off my tank top before stretching out. "I'm super sweaty. I had to take off my top. I have yoga pants on, but they're kind of hot."

"Keep going."

"Do you want me to take those off, too?" I asked, my nervous voice squeaking at the end.

"God, yes." His voice wasn't the slightest bit hesitant. It was low and rough and impossibly sexy.

I wriggled out of my pants. "Okay, then. There go the yoga pants."

"Mmm. That's better. What else?"

"Wait. You haven't told me what you're wearing. And where are you? Are you on the bed?"

"I am. I'm wearing a black t-shirt and I was wearing jeans, but I took them off."

I shut my eyes and conjured the visual—his lean legs, his tempting stomach, his irresistible chest. "Take off your shirt. I love it when you aren't wearing one." I sucked in a long breath, my shoulders rose to my ears as I imagined stretching out next to him, digging into his hair, his tender lips all over me. My chest ached at how much I missed him.

"I'll take everything off if you will."

"Deal." I set the phone next to me and ditched my undies and workout bra in a pile next to the bed, thankful that Max had no idea what was going on. "I'm back."

"Good. I didn't want to start without you." He cleared his throat lustily, which sent a thrill through me. "Where are your hands, Katie?"

I was about to answer, but realized that the leading questions made this so hot. "Where do you want them?"

He groaned. "Your breasts."

I placed my palm on my chest, my nipple responding to both my touch and his voice as it puckered. "They're there. I'm imagining your lips on them, your tongue. It feels incredible." My fingers traced delicate circles against the taut flesh.

"I can taste your skin right now. It's making my cock throb just thinking about it. I want to know if you're wet."

My palm smoothed over the plane of my stomach as I rolled my head to the side. I didn't have to reach my destination to know that just the thought of him had my juices flowing. Heat settled between my legs. Still, I was surprised when my fingers ventured between the tender folds. "Dripping." I proceeded with tiny circles, arching my back. "I want you. I need you."

His breaths were heavy. "Tell me what you want."

"I want to make you happy. I want you in my mouth." The tide was steadily rising as my fingers continued to circle in the slickness. I lightened my touch, teasing to draw out the pleasure. "Can you feel my lips on your dick?"

He groaned again, deeper and more forceful than before. "I love it when you suck me. Everything you do with your tongue is so hot. Jesus, Katie. The shower in Miami. That was the best blowjob I've ever had."

My lips hummed with pride. "I can make your eyes roll into the back of your head if you let me."

"Oh, God. I want to be inside you."

Desperation took root in my body, craving his words just as much as I wanted his touch. "Make love to me." My hips bucked against my hand and I went faster and harder.

"You know I want to. Uhhhh. I can feel you around me." His voice grew guttural and he drew out his words. "You're so tight around my cock. How do you want it?"

I turned my head against the pillow and cradled the phone between my ear and shoulder. My free hand trailed down my stomach and I slipped a finger inside my slick opening. "Be slow with me. I want to feel every inch of your cock." My mind swirled with thoughts of his careful thrusts and I clamped my eyelids tighter, not wanting to leave the world in my head, where I was with him again.

"Oh, God, Katie. Come with me."

"Just a minute. I'm close. Talk to me."

"Do you remember the day we met?"

"I do." My tongue ran along my lips.

"I had a hard-on all day. It hurt to keep it in my pants. I just wanted to take down your ponytail and have you on that big table in your studio."

"Tell me more." I increased the pressure with my fingers, rolling back and forth across my clit.

"I couldn't stop staring at your breasts in that little black top. I would have torn it off you if I could have. And your ass. I almost went off in my pants every time you bent over to pick up a camera lens."

I let my fingers laze over the tight bundle of nerves. It felt so good to hear him talk about me that way. "You had the funniest look on your face that day. I had to tell you to stop. Remember?"

He laughed, quietly. "I couldn't stop looking at you. And

when we talked afterward, that was when I knew I was in trouble. You were so smart and funny and sexy. I've never wanted a woman the way I want you."

I gasped, but not from the physical sensation. His words were more than my body could take. My skin flooded with warmth, my shoulders froze, my mind spun with thoughts of him and desire and opening my heart.

"You're almost there, aren't you?" he asked.

"Yes, hurry." My hands worked faster and with purpose as my breaths sputtered between my lips.

"Oh, God." His voice was ragged and deep. "I'm there, Katie."

"Me too."

I heard him call out just as my body clutched and released, over and over again, shuddering in steady waves. My chest heaved as I sucked in necessary air, my head became wonderfully fuzzy. Relief took me floating back to earth. I sank into the bed, rocking my head on the pillow.

"Peter?" I asked between breaths. "Are you there?"

"Just barely. Jesus. That was hot."

"Smoking hot." I bit my lip, taking delight at losing my phone-sex virginity, quite the naughty milestone.

"I miss you so much. It feels like next Saturday is never going to get here." He blew out an exhalation. "Listen to me. I sound like a kid."

"No, it's sweet. I love it when you're sweet." My eyes began to mist, my inescapable reaction to him. "I miss you, too."

CHAPTER TEN

"EVERY DAY?" Gwen asked.

I grinned, cradling the phone on my shoulder as I dried some silverware. "A dozen, every day." In all honesty, I'd been wondering if perhaps Peter would eventually send me every lavender rose in the tristate area.

"Does he say the same thing on the card every time?"

I stifled a laugh. That morning's bouquet came with a note asking if I'd had a chance to stock up on loofahs. "No, he says different things."

"Like what? And why are you giggling?"

"I don't know. It's all sweet and romantic." I stopped short of more, wanting to keep Peter's sentiments to myself. Those notes were our secret, our silly inside jokes, and that made me feel closer to him. It was a poor substitute for the real thing, but it was something. "Is that good enough?"

"Not really, but you're entitled to be secretive. I have to say I'm impressed that you aren't freaking out yet."

I pursed my lips. "I think I'm doing really well." The truth was that talking on the phone was easy. Aside from overcoming a few jitters about phone sex, it had been effortless. I was still nervous about what would happen when I saw him again, as eager as I was for it to happen. Would it be as amazing as it had been in Miami or was that just the excitement of something new? Would he still want me when saw me again? The way he wanted me in Miami?

"So what are you going to do for Peter? I mean, in exchange for the flowers, aside from the obvious. Sexual favors and whatnot."

"Cute. Real cute. I actually made a print for him. It's beautiful."

"What's it a picture of?"

"I went through everything from the day I photographed the band. I found one shot of him that's breathtaking." My voice caught in my throat. "I converted it to black and white and layered it with one of my New York photos that he said he liked. I hope he likes it. I sent it to arrive at his hotel tomorrow morning."

"Sounds serious."

"It's just a print." In reality, I'd spent hours on it, most often distracted by the beauty of his features. "I wanted to do something. He's so sweet to me."

"It's not an accusation. You made him a gift. That sounds serious to me." Gwen said something off the line and I could hear another voice in the background. "Katie, I'm sorry. I gotta go. Ted's got dinner ready."

"Back to the normal Sunday routine? That's good."

"We're hanging in there," she said, plainly hedging her answer. "Hey, are we still on for dinner Friday?"

"Of course. Wouldn't miss it."

———

PETER CALLED me late that night after they'd played.

"How was the show?" I asked.

"What can I say? Cleveland rocks. What'd you do all night?"

"Answered email, checked in on Mrs. G downstairs and ate ice cream for dinner."

He groaned. "Sometimes I think you're trying to torture me. I eat ice cream for dinner all the time at home. It's harder to get away with it on the road. People look at you funny."

I grinned and curled up on the couch, where Max soon joined me. "Not everyone can appreciate the benefits of such a meal."

"What's your favorite flavor? Wait. Don't tell me. I want to guess. Hmm..."

I giggled. "Don't overthink it."

"Strawberry. No, I'm thinking you're more complicated than that. Mocha almond fudge."

"Nice try. Mint chocolate chip."

"Dammit. Bet you can't guess mine."

"Rocky Road," I answered without hesitation. It just seemed like the obvious answer.

"That's cheating. You didn't even stop to think about it."

"Am I right?" I rolled to my back, which annoyed Max, but he quickly settled on my stomach.

"Yes. You're right. It's been my favorite since I was a kid. I used to beg my mom to buy it, but we didn't always have money for things like that."

"Do your parents still live in Chicago?"

"I moved them out to the suburbs a few years ago. I put them through the wringer when I was growing up. I figured it was the least I could do."

"You bought them a house?"

"I did. It's not huge or anything, but it's paid for and my dad has a yard to mess around with. My mom is just happy to have a kitchen where everything works."

"Wow. That's so great," I said, amazed by the scope of his generosity. "My mom still lives in the same house in New Jersey that I grew up in. My dad passed away a few years ago."

"Do you have brothers and sisters?"

"Nope. Only child."

"Me too. Isn't that funny? That we're both only kids? I probably wouldn't have gotten in so much hot water if I'd had a sibling to rat on me."

"Why? What did you do?" I asked, trying to conjure an image of Peter as a teenager.

"Jesus, you name it. Smoking dope, skipping school, vandalism. Stupid-ass shit. My parents both worked all the time, so I was pretty out of control. It wasn't until a friend loaned me a guitar that things turned around. I took to it right away and the rest is history. I guess you could say that music saved me, more or less."

We were both quiet after his admission. The only thing I could hear was the sound of my own breathing. "I think photography saved me, but it was more from suburban mediocrity than anything serious."

"I don't even want to think about what I would be doing if I hadn't picked up a camera."

"I don't want to think about that either. If it wasn't for that camera, I never would've met you."

I immediately knew the other half of the equation. "And if it wasn't for that guitar, I never would've met you," I said quietly. Goose bumps dotted my arms. "Some people would say that's fate."

"What about you, Katie? Do you think its fate that we met? Because I do."

CHAPTER ELEVEN

AFTER A VERY LONG WORKWEEK, Peter sent his usual dozen flowers on Friday, taking me to a grand total of 144 roses. Some had faded, but there were still vases in the bathroom, next to my bed, on the kitchen counter. I'd brought a dozen to Mrs. G, but then she only wanted to hear about the notes he'd sent with them. I had to give her the G-rated version of most. She was sure I was a fool if I didn't beg Peter for an engagement ring the instant he got to town.

"I'm running out of space," I said when he called before Slump's show in Philadelphia. "I can't guarantee there'll be anywhere to sit when you get here tomorrow." I slipped a silver hoop earring in my other ear, getting ready to go out to dinner with Gwen.

"I'm proving a point. And I don't plan on doing any sitting while I'm there."

I smirked at myself in the bathroom mirror and ran my fingers along the edge of the white granite vanity. "What time are you getting here?" My pulse quickened just realizing how close we were to finally seeing each other. There was excitement accompanied by an edge of uncertainty, as I worried that the reality might not live up to everything I'd built in my head.

"We can't bring the bus into the city until right before sound check. That's at three. I'm trying to get out of it, but Elliot has some new song he wants to work on. Maybe you could come and watch. It would be boring, but we could torture each other with knowing glances."

My cheeks flushed and I laughed. "Okay. Well, we can talk tomorrow morning and work it out. I should go. Gwen hates it when I'm late." I grabbed my purse and keys, wondering, for what felt like the hundredth time, how I'd been lucky enough to find him.

"Say hi from me. Miss you."

"Miss you too. Have a good show."

I ran down the stairs and hopped in a cab, even though I probably should have walked the twelve blocks to the restaurant, a little Spanish place with the best sangria, a favorite spot for girls' night. Only a minute or two behind schedule, I'd still arrived after Gwen. She sat at a round table in the center of the dining room, an enormous pitcher filled with red wine and slices of orange and apple before her.

The restaurant was packed and noisy, people chattering while glasses clinked and waiters in short red jackets and black pants maneuvered through the small space. Gwen's face held no enthusiasm. She was usually psyched for girls' night, but she looked as though she'd just come from a funeral.

"Hey, honey. What's up?" I asked, looping my bag over the back of the chair and pecking her on the cheek.

She stared at me. "You should pour yourself a drink first. While you're at it, I'll take a refill." She slid a chunky blue glass goblet to my side of the table.

The fruit sloshed into the glass along with the sangria and I took a long sip. "Talk to me. What's going on? You were fine when we talked this afternoon."

"Ted and I broke up."

"Oh my God. Are you serious?"

"He got it in his head that I have something going on with one of the doctors at the hospital. He just wouldn't let it go."

I leaned closer to her. "You don't have something going on with a doctor, do you?"

She bugged her eyes at me. "No."

"How did you leave it with Ted?"

"He's out drinking with his buddies. They're going to a strip club." She kneaded her forehead. "You know, maybe this is for the best. Ted and I have been trying to hold it together and maybe we're wrong for each other."

The waiter arrived, putting a temporary stop to our conversation. I ordered my usual shrimp paella, my mind scrambling for words to help Gwen. Relationship advice wasn't my strong suit. *This is all wrong.* Gwen was the stable one, the girl with the long-term boyfriend, the happily-ever-after type. If Gwen couldn't make it work, how could I ever accomplish the feat?

I reached across the table for her hand. "I don't think that's true. You guys are great together. You just have some things to work out."

She snatched a hunk of bread from the basket and ripped it in half. "You know what's really sad? I'm sick of working things out. Like seriously sick of it."

"Oh."

A torrent of emotion flooded out of Gwen—sadness and anger, determination and resignation. It was like watching her go through every stage of grieving in a single sitting.

We took our second pitcher of sangria to a spot at the end of the bar after we'd finished eating. Gwen still wanted to talk and the restaurant had reservations to seat.

My phone rang but I let it go to voicemail.

Moments later, it rang a second time.

"Just answer it. I have to pee anyway," Gwen said, getting up from her barstool.

I dug around in my purse and my heart skipped when I saw Peter's name on the caller ID. "Hey," I said. "Don't you have a show to play?"

"We go on in a few minutes. I have a question. Is it okay if I come tonight?"

I blinked several times. "What? Of course it's okay, but I thought you were staying in Philly."

"I called a car service. I wouldn't get to your place until one or two in the morning. I can't wait anymore."

I cradled the phone closer as if his hand was in mine while I watched an unsteady Gwen walk back from the bathroom. "I can't wait anymore either. I'll wait up for you."

I slid my phone back into my bag, trying to disguise the smile on my face. This was not the time to be happy around Gwen, but she surprised me with a sneaky grin.

"It was Peter wasn't it?" She slapped my leg and watched as my face gave me away. "I knew it. What did he say? When do you get to see him tomorrow?" She leaned closer, the smell of one too many glasses of sangria washing over me. "Are you two even going to leave your apartment while he's here? You're going to spend all of your time fucking, aren't you?"

A breathy laugh escaped my lips. "Yes, it was him. He's coming to the city tonight. He won't get in until late."

The expression on her face softened and she dropped her head to the side, although that could also have been because she was a bit wobbly. "That's great. You two are so cute together. He's clearly smitten."

Smitten? Really? "I should get you in a cab." I rubbed her arm and put down a five-dollar bill for the bartender. "You're tipsy."

She frowned, jutting out her lower lip. "Yeah. I guess so."

Outside the restaurant, I peered down the street for an available taxi when a thought hit me. "What do I wear for a two a.m. rendezvous at my apartment?"

"With Peter? Uh, nothing."

"Be serious. Isn't that a little presumptuous?" A cab hurtled down the street toward us at record speed.

"Um, no. It's not. Don't mess this up by questioning what's going on. I know you and you doubt every guy. Don't do it."

Of course I doubted every guy. It took a lot of work not to. "I don't want to doubt him. Not Peter. I really don't."

"I'm totally serious. I want this for you, Katie. I want you to be happy and fall in love and all that good stuff. You deserve it."

"You deserve it too." I opened the car door for her and bent down as she climbed inside. "Are you okay? I'm worried about you."

Her eyes grew sad. "I'll be okay. I just need to remember that sometimes things don't work out the way we want them to."

———

Max watched as I nearly wore a channel in the hardwood floor. I looked at the clock again. One forty-three. *Where is he?* The last text he'd sent said ten minutes and that had been twenty minutes ago.

Max had also observed me an hour earlier as I sifted through pajamas and underwear trying to decide what to wear. I decided against Gwen's nude suggestion, since I could easily see myself poking my head out into the hall to discover the pizza delivery guy had the wrong apartment.

Ultimately I decided on a skinny-strapped white tank and a

pair of black silk and lace panties. It was the melding of what I'd once convinced myself I could be, the bold seductress eager to ravage her man, and what I now knew I was, the vulnerable girl terrified to hope that things with Peter were real.

The stage was set in the apartment—lights off, a handful of candles glowing. I'd changed the sheets and fluffed the comforter.

The buzzer sounded and I dashed to the intercom. "Hello?" I asked, as if I didn't know who it was. I covered my mouth when I giggled, bouncing on my toes.

"It's me."

"Come on up." I held the button and opened the door, flitting out into the stairwell to see him, forgetting that I was out there in my undies.

"Hey," he said. He smiled—that undeniable mischievous smile. He none too subtly eyed me, taking the steps two at a time.

I had to stop myself from thundering down the stairs and begging him to take me against the banister.

I pressed my finger to my lips. "Shh."

His dark hair was a mess and he looked tired, but his eyes had an unmistakable sparkle. I grabbed his arm when he was within reach and pulled him into my apartment. The door slammed shut behind us.

He dropped his black duffel bag to the floor and placed his warm hands on my hips, sending a sizzle along my spine. "Hi." He pulled me closer. Even his presence smoldered. "How are you?"

"Great." My eyes fluttered as we pressed together. I fought a disconcerting surprising wave of shyness. "Long car ride?"

Peter flipped my hair over my shoulder and his lips wandered to my neck. "Too long." He placed a single kiss against my skin. Any uncertainty I had went up in smoke.

I clapped my hands on either side of his head. Our lips collided into each other, moving forward with eager, probing tongues. I gathered his t-shirt in my hands and pushed it over his head between kisses.

He liberated me from my tank top in a single motion. "Thank God. No bra," he said. He gripped my rib cage and zeroed in on my breasts with his soft lips and talented tongue.

My hands fingers combed into through his hair. Every movement of his mouth and hands made me feel as if I was going to shoot off like a rocket. I became so disoriented that I caught myself thinking there must be a way I could take his pants off with my feet while standing. A gasp left my lips as he licked the taut skin of my nipple. "Bed."

"Yes." His eyes swept across the expanse of my loft while he kicked off his shoes.

I clutched his hand and we hurried, the faint light of candles glowing around the bed. We tumbled onto the mattress with a whoosh and a bounce, both of us laughing. I crawled backwards on my elbows to the center. My hair splayed out as I sank into the fluffy bedding. He knelt next to me and I unbuttoned and unzipped his jeans. I yanked them down his hips and ran my hand over the bulging ridge in his boxer briefs. He closed his eyes for a second before he had the good sense to simply collapse next to me and shimmy both garments down his legs. He straddled my hips. I reached for his cock, caressing his smooth, throbbing skin.

He descended on my chest with his luscious lips and wet, open-mouth kisses. He glossed my nipples with his tongue. I squirmed beneath him, wanting everything I knew he was capable of, at that instant. My fingers raked through his thick hair as I strained to kiss the top of his head.

I raised my knee and rubbed it against his balls, eliciting a groan. He dropped his full weight on me, fervently kissing me while our tongues tangled. His hands cradled my face as I pressed my palms into his muscular back, hitching my foot beneath the perfect curve of his ass, tugging him closer. His cock rode against my pubic bone through the silky fabric of my panties. I tilted my hips to feel his full length, aching for him as all I did was get hot. And wet.

"Peter," I whispered, distracted by his penetrating eyes. "I can't wait. I want you inside me."

A grin spread across his face. "Thank God. I thought it was just me who was feeling impatient."

"Here," I said, rolling out from under him and crawling to my bedside table. I reached into the drawer and pulled out a condom as I felt him creep up behind me.

He flattened me against the bed and swept my hair from my neck, kissing it and my shoulder as his cock nestled between us. He traced his fingertips from my ribs to my hipbone, even his most delicate touch sending waves of tingles through me. "Mmm. I like seeing you from this angle." He knelt back, dragging his finger along my spine before he warmed the small of my back with his breath, turning anticipation into sweet agony. His hands curled under the waistband of my panties and he slowly slipped them down my legs. I watched over my shoulder.

I twisted to my back and tore open the package before rolling on the condom. "Come here." I caressed the underside of his arm as he maneuvered between my legs.

Our eyes connected as he stroked my slick folds a few times before gliding inside. I held my breath, grappling with the impossibly good feeling of the moment. He kissed me tenderly. His breaths came quick against my lips. The hurried sound only made me need him more. I bucked my hips and he dictated the speed, pushing me harder and faster. Twisting his torso, he hit the perfect spot, creating friction that sizzled through me.

I rocked my hips, meeting him with every stroke and he

nuzzled his face into my neck. We both moaned—speech would be too complicated. Our bodies slid against each other, sweat beading between us. Teetering on the brink, I was clinging to the pressure for dear life. He gave several long and forceful thrusts and called my name. With that, I let go, and the release rippled through me, my shoulders and chest shaking.

Both of us breathless, Peter rolled to my side and immediately pulled me closer, kissing me on top of the head. I spread my hand across his stomach and hooked my ankle around his, resting my head on his shoulder. Contentment settled over me.

"I feel so much better," he said.

I sighed. "I know. Me too."

"Bathroom?" he asked. "I need to get rid of this condom."

"Far end of the apartment. On the other side of the living room."

I rolled on to my stomach and watched him walk away, admiring everything about his unbelievable body, ass near the top of the list.

He smiled when he returned and climbed into bed. "I missed you so much." He combed his fingers through my hair. "I felt like I was going crazy."

"I missed you, too."

Max hopped up onto the bed. "Shit," Peter said, jerking his head.

"Oh, God. I'm sorry. This is Max. Are you allergic?"

He blew out an exhalation before reaching out for Max's head and stroking. "No. I love cats. He just surprised me."

Max rubbed his cheek against the back of Peter's hand, purring loudly.

"Huh." I jutted out my lower lip and looked at Peter. "He doesn't usually like strangers."

"Max will be my best friend by the time I leave."

I suddenly realized that after two nights, he'd be gone again.

I'd been so focused on getting to Saturday. The future beyond tomorrow night was out of focus at best and I might end up back at square one when he was gone.

Max turned in a few circles and settled down next to Peter. "How long have you had him?" he asked, again stroking Max's fur. "I wish I could have a pet. It's impossible when you're on the road all the time."

"Max is almost three." My voice was tinged with melancholy. "My ex gave him to me the Christmas we got engaged. He's basically the only good thing Brad gave me."

"Ah, the ex." Peter wrapped his other arm around me. "Will you tell me more about what happened? I want to understand what made you swear off relationships for so long."

"It's not a complicated story, it's just a little pathetic." I swallowed in an attempt to prevent tears. "We were together for two years and about to be married when he left. He fell in love with a woman he worked with. I'd thought there was something going on between them for months, but he always denied it and said that they were just friends. Turned out my hunch was correct."

"So you had to cancel the wedding, the honeymoon. The whole thing."

"My mom and I had to call every single person we invited to tell them it was off. I almost think it was harder on her than it was on me. Although I was pretty numb at the time." I sniffled, which I hated doing. "So I ate ice cream and chocolate for a month and then I decided to stop feeling sorry for myself."

"I wouldn't say you were feeling sorry for yourself. He changed your whole life. Of course, I think a paper cut is a good reason to eat ice cream, so I'm probably not the person to ask."

My index finger swept his hair from his forehead, where I placed a kiss. "You are the sweetest man. Really."

He grinned and kissed me on the lips. "I try."

"So, yeah, that's it. From there, I focused on my career and figured my love life could just go on the back burner for a really long time."

"You had to know that would never work."

"It wasn't my best idea ever." I ran my fingers through the hair of his chest. "Sometimes people break your heart. You know that. You told me you had a really bad breakup."

"It was awful." He cleared his throat. "The difference being that I was the jerk."

"No way. You're such a sweetheart."

"No, I'm pretty sure I acted like an asshole."

"What happened?"

He settled his head on to the pillow and I folded myself into him. "This was with Susie, my first serious girlfriend. I really loved her. Remember, I didn't have my first girlfriend until I was nineteen."

"I still don't get that. I love you in your glasses. I totally would've dated you in high school." I kissed his chest.

"Thanks. You're definitely in the minority." He kneaded his forehead. "Are you sure you want to hear this?"

"Yes."

"This was right when the band was starting to take off. I got really swept up in everything the first time we did a big tour. People are stroking your ego and there's a party every night and women start throwing themselves at you. Like I said, Susie was my first serious girlfriend, but she was also my first, period."

"Oh."

"And so, yeah, I slept with some girl after a show one night. I felt guilty the next day, but I just started drinking instead of dealing with it. I ended up with a different girl the next night. After that, I couldn't deal with the guilt anymore and I told Susie everything and she dumped me."

"Oh, God. I'm sorry."

"No, don't be sorry. It was my fault. I fucked up, big-time.

Believe me, I spent months and months kicking myself. I'm never making that mistake again." He brushed my chin with his fingertip and gazed into my eyes. "I told myself that if I ever found the right woman, I would never let her get away."

My shoulders relaxed and heat flooded my cheeks. "That's good to know."

His thumb gently traced my jaw. "I think I'm falling in love with you."

My heart fluttered, I smiled and blinked like crazy, but I was speechless. *The "L" word.* I hadn't heard that in a long time and as terrifying as it was to admit, it sounded amazing coming from his incredible lips. He scanned my face, undoubtedly looking for an answer.

Fear cast aside, swept up in the moment, I told him. "I know I'm falling in love with you."

CHAPTER TWELVE

MAX WAS WHOLLY annoyed that I didn't get out of bed until after ten a.m. He'd been meowing and head-butting my hand for an hour, begging me to get up and feed him.

"Duty calls," I said, rolling over to kiss Peter on the temple. I threw back the sheets and tiptoed into the kitchen.

"Sweetie, you could start a nude pet-sitting business," he mumbled sleepily. "In case the photography thing doesn't work out."

I scooped the food into Max's bowl and refilled his water dish as Max rubbed up against my leg. "You might need to rethink the business model." I turned to see Peter put on his glasses before he patted my spot on the mattress. He looked good enough to eat, his chest tempting me from across the room, hair a complete disaster. I traipsed back toward the bed but stopped short. "Don't move."

He flattened his hand on the mattress and furrowed his brow in confusion. "What?"

"I'm serious. Don't move," I called out as I jogged into the other room. Returning with one of my cameras, I removed the lens cap and began taking pictures. "The light is just perfect on you right now. You look amazing."

His shoulders visibly relaxed. "I do? Because you look spectacular holding a camera with no clothes on."

I snapped away, studying his features as I captured something new with every frame—the curious bump on his nose, the tiny crinkles at the corners of his eyes when he was happy. "There was no time to get dressed. I couldn't miss this light." The structure of his jaw was particularly mesmerizing, but the smile that played at his lips was a close second. "Seriously. You're so handsome." I was aware of every breath as it left and entered my lungs. "It boggles the mind."

His cheeks flushed pink as he took off his glasses and pinched the bridge of his nose. "Stop taking my picture and get over here."

"No way. Just a few more." I moved to the other side of the bed and crouched closer, capturing more of the depth to his steely blue eyes now that he was no longer wearing his glasses. "Your eyes are incredible."

He sat up and confronted the lens. "How are they now?"

"Actually, they look sort of mysterious when you do that." I pulled the camera away from my face. "Is this really making you that uncomfortable?" I went back to snapping away, moving to the end of the bed again. "Because this is what I do, you know." I took two more shots. "Damn, the light's gone already."

"Thank God. Will you come back to bed now?"

I replaced the lens cap and set the camera on the bedside table before climbing in next to him. "I got some really great stuff." I leaned down, kissing him, drinking in the soft brush of his lips. "I might have to make you another print since you liked the first one I gave you so much."

"I loved it, but I'd rather have one of you." He pulled me

down on top of him and gazed up into my eyes, smoothing my hair back from my face. "Come on the road with me."

"What?" I rolled to my side. Had he really said that?

He took my hand. "Come on the road with me. Can you take off a week or two? Rearrange your schedule?"

I sat frozen for a moment, expecting my old panicky mindset to kick in, but I took a breath, allowing a remarkable calm to stay. Maybe I really was ready for this. Maybe enough time had passed for me to heal. "I might be able to do a week." My mind rummaged through my upcoming schedule. "Any longer and I'd have to leave for a few days in the middle. I know I have one big shoot coming up that keeps getting rescheduled. Wait. I thought girlfriends were banned from the bus."

He grinned with mischievous satisfaction. "Girlfriend. I like the sound of that." He smoothed his hand over my butt, just as Max made his presence known on the bed with a meow. "I'd rent our own bus. Elliot used to do it all the time when he was married. It'd take a day or two to arrange, but you could fly and meet us in Toronto or Detroit."

"Ooh, Detroit. That does sound tempting." I smiled as he stuck his tongue out at me. "How do you know I'm not going to drive you crazy?"

"I already know you drive me crazy. I'd love to be that crazy every day if I can." He nuzzled my neck and I turned my hip into his. "We would have tons of downtime, all alone, nothing but a bed and a kitchen and satellite TV."

"Wi-fi? I have to be able to get online for work."

"Of course."

I gave the doubting part of my brain one more minute to come up with some ridiculous reason I shouldn't do it. "Sounds perfect."

"Really?"

"Yes."

He flashed his eyes and made a throaty sound, rolling me to my back and hovering above me. "I love hearing you say that word."

After a very hot twenty minutes of "yes", ending with more time in the shower, Peter and I got dressed and headed out for lunch at a coffee shop down the street. We sat in the back. He wore his sunglasses to avoid being noticed. We held hands and ate big, fat deli sandwiches and french fries. After he paid the check, we strolled back to my apartment and I leaned my head against his shoulder as we walked. It felt as if we were starring in one of those wonderfully funny and romantic movies set in New York like *Annie Hall*. So perfect.

Mrs. Gunderson was at her mailbox when we came in through the front door. "Oh, Katie," she said. "This must be the young man I've heard so much about."

I bugged my eyes at her, but couldn't hide my smile as Peter swiped his sunglasses from his face and shook her hand. I made the introductions.

Mrs. Gunderson scrutinized Peter with the narrowest of stares. "She's a lovely girl, Peter."

"So I noticed." He squeezed my shoulder and kissed my temple.

"I love her like a daughter," Mrs. G continued. "She deserves a fellow who will prove to her that men aren't all the same."

"He's a great guy, Mrs. G. And I love you, too." I leaned over to give her a kiss on the cheek, surprised she'd given Peter a hard time at all. She'd been so won-over by the flowers, but perhaps seeing him in person reminded her just how hurt I had once been. "I'm really glad you two had a chance to meet. It's important to me that you like each other."

"I just want what's best for you," she said, giving in to half of a smile.

"Mrs. Gunderson might not be my biggest fan," Peter said when we got back to my apartment. "Maybe I should send her some Slump CDs. Grease the wheels, so to speak." He pulled me closer.

I laughed, quietly. "She's anxious for me to find the right guy. And she likes you. Really, she does. She was very impressed with the flowers. I gave her some of the overflow."

Peter's gaze traveled to the living room. Max's favorite gray couch was largely obscured by the coffee table laden with roses.

"I guess I did go a little overboard, didn't I?" He wrapped his arms around me. "I was only trying to send a message. I didn't want you to think I just hooked up with you in Miami."

I became aware of every breath as my chest rose and fell and our foreheads rested against each other. "I got the message. Loud and clear." We kissed for a moment and Max rudely intruded, meowing and rubbing against our legs. We both crouched to pet him, which only seemed to whet his thirst for affection.

Peter glanced at his watch. "Shit. It's almost three."

I plopped onto the floor and rubbed Max's ears. "You need to get to sound check, don't you? That sucks."

Peter pulled his phone from his pocket. "You know what? They don't need me. One of the guitar techs can do my check."

"Are you sure? Don't do that on my account."

"Yes, I'm sure," he said, pressing the keypad on his phone. "I don't want to give up two hours with you." He walked over to the couch and sat with his arm across the back. "Hey, Tony, can you get one of the techs to do my guitar check for me? I'm super busy." He winked at me before his eyes narrowed. "Are you serious? Fine. Put him on." A booming voice came on to the line—I could hear it from across the room. Peter rolled his eyes.

"Elliot, chill out. We'll work on the new song tomorrow night in Boston. It's not that big of a deal. It's not like we were going to play it tonight." He shook his head. "You know what? She's my girlfriend and I want to spend time with her. Is that so wrong? You and Stony pull this kind of shit all the time and I never say anything. So just deal with it. I'll be there an hour before we go on." He pushed another button on his phone and tossed it onto the couch.

"You didn't have to do that." I hated feeling like I might be causing a problem. "Seriously. If you need to go, you should go. Don't get into a thing with Elliot just because of me."

He got up and walked toward me, reaching for my hand and pulling me back to standing. "Fuck Elliot. You are way more important to me right now."

———

WHEN IT WAS time to head to the club, we took the Town Car Peter had arranged. We leaned against each other in the back-seat and held hands, our fingers intertwined. Neither of us said a thing for a stretch. Silence. Comfortable silence. I didn't need to talk and apparently neither did he. We could just be. Together. Never before had I reached the point in a relationship where silence wasn't uncomfortable.

I peered up at Peter. He grinned and kissed me on the fore-head, allowing his lips to linger. The city breezed by through the windows—clusters of people on the sidewalk, a hot dog cart, a stretch of construction scaffolding and the rickety wood pedestrian tunnel beneath.

"I love this city," I muttered, shifting in my seat and snuggling closer to him.

"It's pretty awesome. We love coming to play here. Not sure I could ever live here though. I've been in Chicago my whole life."

"I like Chicago," I said, my voice fading. I'd been to Chicago several times for photo shoots and I thought it was fun, but I stubbornly clung to my Manhattan Visitor's Bureau attitude. There's no real reason to live anywhere else.

Peter directed the driver back behind the club and ushered me through the congestion of equipment trucks to the place where Slump's two massive black tour buses sat idling. Elliot stood talking to a pair of women outside one of the bus doors. The three of them spotted us as we approached and the women hustled up to Peter, CDs and Sharpies in hand, asking for autographs. Elliot seemed noticeably annoyed as he trailed behind them.

One of the girls was spilling out of her top, jiggling and tittering as she rambled on to Peter. "Oh, my God. My sister has been totally in love with you forever. She would die if she knew I met you."

Peter nodded and smiled, signed her CD and handed it back to her.

The second fan tried a different approach, speaking in a phony intellectual voice. "You guys are my favorite band in the whole world. I listen to your music and it's so moving. I feel like I really understand you guys. This is the third show we've seen on this tour. We're driving up to Toronto too." She continued watching as he signed a stack of CDs, very noticeably rubbing her breast against his upper arm.

I fought a strong urge to throw my arms around him and mark my territory by kissing him with reckless abandon. Taking a deep breath to collect myself, I crossed my arms across my chest. Jealousy was admittedly my worst personality trait and it hadn't been tested in years. But I was older now, no longer the insecure twit I'd been when I was with Brad.

Elliot smiled smugly as the two girls returned to his side. "Yo, Pete, we need to talk about the sound check thing today."

He cocked an eyebrow and nodded in my direction, as if I was the source of the problem.

Now my blood was boiling in a new way. *Asshole. I'm not some idiotic groupie.*

"Ignore him," Peter said when they walked away. "Come on, I want to show you the band bus. So you can see our setup for when you come on the road. I'll spare you the crew bus. It's pretty gross."

Peter led the way up the steep stairs. "This is where we spend most of our time."

We walked into a seating area with long, upholstered bench seats, a pair of recliners and a flat-screen. Beyond that was a dining table between two more benches and a small kitchen next to it. I'd been on plenty of tour buses over the last several years, but this one was extra swanky, with rope lights illuminating the somewhat cheesy décor.

Peter pointed at the mini-fridge. "Do you want anything?"

I shook my head. "I'm good."

"You can't do much in the way of cooking in the kitchen, but we'll stock it with snacks." He traced his fingers down my spine and wrapped his hand around my hip.

It was exciting to think about the great adventure ahead of us, but I felt uneasy too. Maybe this was too much, too soon.

I had an unwelcome flashback to the day Brad showed me the apartment he'd picked out for us. He thought it was perfect, a renovated unit, everything brand new and shiny. I'd been hoping for a cool old brownstone with original woodwork and a fireplace. I'd asked if we could keep looking, he'd insisted that his choice was perfect, and that we would be happy there for a very long time. I should have known right then that it was never going to work.

Peter pushed back a pocket door to show me the postage-stamp bathroom. "Don't worry, you won't have to shower in here. That's why we get hotel rooms every day."

I nodded and he took my hand and I followed past a few bunks and into the back. "And this is the bedroom." He pulled me into an embrace and shut the door behind us. His mouth went to my jaw and I closed my eyes to get my bearings. "I love the way you smell, Katie." He pecked at my neck, taking a gentle nibble of my ear. "I wish we had time for this. You're getting me all worked-up."

"Me?" I asked, shaking my head. "I'm pretty sure you started it."

Peter grinned and brushed his lips against mine. "I admit it. It's all my fault."

When we stepped off the bus, we were greeted by another small cluster of fans asking to have CDs and posters signed. Peter obliged, being polite and posing for a photo while I stood to the side and waited.

We then made our way through the back door of the club. Peter grabbed the first crew guy we ran into. "Hey, Mo. I want you to meet my girlfriend, Katie. Can you tell Hunter that I need an all-access laminate for her? Right away."

We continued down the hall to the band's dressing room. "Just ignore Elliot if he's being a dick," Peter mumbled into my ear.

Mo strode toward us with my credentials. "Here you go, man. Anything else?"

Peter looped the lanyard over my neck. "Make sure she has whatever she wants tonight. And can you make sure the dressing room bathroom isn't disgusting? I don't want her having to deal with that."

I smiled sheepishly, fully recovered from my minor panic on the bus. It was so adorable to have him want to take care of me. He took my hand and we stepped into the dressing room, the same set-up as Miami, with a similar array of girls hanging around.

One woman stood out among them all, with long, sleek black hair, full red lips and impeccable, radiant skin. She had to be a model—her exotic brown eyes and perfect posture were annoyingly breathtaking. She'd perched herself on the arm of a chair next to Stony, rubbing his shoulder and smiling at him as they talked.

She turned and looked at us, her face lighting up like a beacon when she saw Peter.

He strode over to her and gave her an embrace that seemed a beat or two too long from where I was standing. "Sasha," he said. "It's so great to see you. Can't believe you missed the show in DC. We had a killer party."

Stony didn't seem to care that his bimbo and Peter had taken such great interest in each other. Sasha flipped her shiny hair over her shoulder and held on to Peter's arm. Every millisecond with her hand on him felt as though it was an eternity.

He turned to me. "Katie, this is Sasha."

Sasha continued to hold on to him, her fingers pressed against the bare skin of his arm. "Hi," she said, in the snottiest tone I could imagine. To her, I was probably just unwanted competition. "So, Peter, tell me about the party in DC. Did Amber show up? She told me she was going."

My insides knotted as I listened to them chat, Peter laughing at something she said. I'd gone from feeling as though I was his prized princess to a third wheel. He hadn't even introduced me as his girlfriend.

One of the roadies stuck his head in the room. "I need everybody to clear out. Band goes on in ten minutes."

Peter kissed Sasha on the cheek and said, "Please tell me you're going to be here after the show. I'd love to catch up some more." He then turned back to me. "Mo should be out in the hall. Ask him to walk you to the side of the stage." He gave me the same peck on the cheek that he'd given to Sasha. "I'm sorry. I'd do it myself, but I didn't realize how close it was to showtime."

Trying to hold my head high and let things roll off my back, I found Mo and he was happy to escort me, only after we waited for Sasha since she was apparently coming along too. *Great.* She and I said nothing to each other as we followed Mo, the awkwardness hanging in the air like a thick cloud.

We stood waiting in the wings before the band went on, the NYC crowd much louder and more animated than the one in Miami. Sasha was a few feet away from me, applying lipstick while looking in a compact mirror. Inferiority washed over me and I felt as if I was a teenager again, exactly the way it felt to stand next to one of the beautiful, popular girls in the school bathroom. I remembered what it was like to think no boy would ever like me, that no guy would ever even notice I existed.

The band came up behind us and my heart flip-flopped at the sight of Peter winking, but then it dragged when he waved at Sasha too.

It was a struggle to enjoy the set, my whole body on edge from the mere presence of Sasha. *What is my fucking problem? She's just some random girl he knows. Big deal. He asked me to go on the road with him.* I focused on the rock 'n' roll version of Peter coming to life. I focused on simply refusing to acknowledge my fears and insecurities. *Those things don't help me. I'm stronger than that.* I focused on my need for oxygen when I caught myself holding my breath.

Two hours later, as the band finished their second encore, I was no less agitated. My skin bristled, my neck ached and my stomach had soured. *We just need to get out of here. Then I'll be fine. Fresh air, a night together and it will all be back to the way it was.*

Peter dashed off after the set saying he really needed to pee and I made my way back to the dressing room by myself. Sasha had disappeared when the band finished and the pettiest parts of me hoped she'd come down with a horrible case of the stomach flu.

Mo stood guard at the dressing room door and informed a handful of other women and me that we would need to wait ten minutes or so until the band finished changing clothes. I considered asking for an exception, reminding Mo that I was a girlfriend and not a groupie, but I also knew that it would be in my best interest to befriend the crew when I went on tour, so I kept quiet.

After a few minutes, the dressing room door swung open and you could hear the sound of the many voices inside. Elliot grabbed the brunette closest to him and pulled her into the room. Everyone else pressed ahead and I got stuck behind the rest of the pack. I approached, anxious to get Peter and leave as soon as possible. That's when I saw them through the crowded room, Peter and Sasha sitting next to each other on a couch. Her hand was on his knee. She was talking animatedly and he was laughing. He put his arm around her, pulled her close, and kissed her forehead.

Oh, God. This is what it's going to be like. Me fighting with other women for him. I can't do this.

CHAPTER THIRTEEN

I'M NOT GOING *to cry. I'm not going to cry. For fuck's sake, don't cry.*

The radio in the cab played awful mariachi music and it felt as if my head weighed fifty pounds, as if I were wearing one of those mascot costume heads. I begged the driver to get me home as quickly as possible, but we got stuck at every red light imaginable. Sitting in traffic, the idling taxi rumbling, my phone buzzed with a text.

Where are you?

I stuffed my phone in my bag and struggled for air. I'd done what I'd known I wasn't ready for and it hit me like a ton of bricks. I'd walked right into it. I should have left it all in Miami where it belonged. *You aren't built for this. You aren't built for love.* The tears rolled down my cheeks and I swept them away with the back of my hand as if that would erase the collateral damage of allowing Peter into my heart.

Unwilling to wait for change, I left the driver with a ridiculous tip. I stole away into my building and flew up the stairs, collapsing against the door once I was inside, sliding all the way to the floor.

My head went between my knees as my lips quivered and shook. My cell phone rang and my heart sank to my stomach when I saw Peter's name on the caller ID. *I can't talk to you. I can't hear you tell me that you have a thing for that woman. I can't hear you tell me you ever did.*

My phone beeped, announcing that I had a message. I stared at the screen, debating what to do, when I got a text.

Where are you? Mo thought he saw you leave.

I chewed on my fingernail. *Fuck. What do I say?* I held my phone to my forehead and it beeped with another text.

Worried. Did you go home?

Max hopped down from my bed and sauntered over to me, his tail waving in the air. He rubbed against my leg, flopped down on the floor and began giving himself a bath. I kicked off my shoes and tucked my knees under my chin. *It's okay. Breathe. You're going to be fine.*

Still worried. Please answer. Are you ok?

I cursed my phone. I cursed Peter's boundless capacity for sweetness. This wasn't going to play out as things had with Brad. Peter actually had the balls to tell me to my face or at least over the phone that he'd found someone else. His words haunted me. He'd said he wouldn't let the right girl get away again. He'd never actually said that I was that girl. I'd been stupid to assume that I might be.

Still worried. Coming to your place.

I buried my face in my hands. I had to reply. *Don't. This won't work.*

Too late. In cab. What does that mean?

Can't deal with the groupie thing.

My phone rang—Peter again. I let it go to voicemail. I decided the real reason that this was so difficult was because I wasn't actually angry with him, or at least not that much. This was all me. I was pissed at myself for letting him get too close, knowing I couldn't handle it. I wasn't ready for this yet.

Please answer. You are freaking me out. Groupie thing?

My heart pounded and I longed for a fast-forward button, just get past this, let him go on his way and leave me alone to try to get over him. I was going to have to start the process of falling out of love. Again. Talking to him wouldn't solve a thing, it would only give me one more memory that would be impossible to erase from my brain.

Tell cab to turn around. You obviously like her.

Too late. I'm here. Who are you talking about???

I got up to my feet and tiptoed to one of the tall windows overlooking the street. I peered down from behind the curtain and there he was, standing in the middle of the sidewalk, phone in one hand, looking directly at my window. He shrugged and his eyes pleaded with me. He pointed at the door and stepped out of sight, ringing the buzzer a second later.

Fuck. I ran over to the intercom and pressed the button. "It's okay. You don't need to tell me to my face that you want to be with Sasha. I get it."

The intercom buzzed.

Fuck.

The intercom buzzed.

I pressed the button to speak. "Please stop buzzing."

My phone beeped and I pulled it from my pocket.

Not leaving. Sasha is a friend. Nothing more.

I'd heard that one before. That was exactly what Brad had told me about Misty, the woman he ran off with. The woman he married two months ago. Exactly the same excuse, word for word. A friend. Stop being so flipping paranoid, she's just a friend. Except that Misty was far more than that.

She looked like more than a friend.

I didn't get an immediate response, and I wondered if I'd

convinced him. Thirsty, I dragged my feet into the kitchen for a glass of water. The ice cream called to me from the freezer, but I swore I wasn't going to fall back into old self-destructive patterns. I had to learn from this. I had to continue to grow and be a better person. Gwen had been right about one thing. I was going to be alone for my entire life if I didn't find a way to get over my trust issues. She'd been wrong about the timing, clearly I wasn't ready for a relationship, but her overall idea was a good one. I had to let life happen.

My phone beeped again.

Sasha is Tony's sister. Have known her forever. Not leaving. Will stay all night.

I crinkled my forehead. *His sister? But she's gorgeous and he's a Neanderthal.* I sighed, in no way comforted by his answer.

His sister?

Yes. His sister.

I groaned as my stomach sank. Idiot. How could I be more of an idiot?

See how fucked up I am? Run while you can.

You are not fucked up. You just think you are.

Before I had the chance to correct him, he sent more.

Not running. Staying.

I blew out a noisy exhalation.

Save yourself. Go to Boston.

You can't hide forever. I ate the mint chocolate chip.

I strode back into the kitchen, opened the freezer, and slammed it shut.

I can live without ice cream.

You sure? I'll wait.

I crept back to the window and sure enough, there he stood with his arms crossed, leisurely pacing in front of the building. My heart was unbearably heavy. I didn't have the strength to carry it around anymore. I watched him—knowing I might not ever find a better guy, someone patient, understanding and funny. He'd even told me that he was falling in love with me.

I went to my closet and changed into pajama pants and a tank top. I trudged back to the other side of the loft and flopped onto the bed. *He said he was falling in love with me and I'm messing it up by being a psychotic bitch who isn't capable of getting out of her own head.* My eyes fluttered shut, but the only image I was left with was Peter—his electric smile, those smoldering blue eyes, kissable lips. I could see him laughing, making fun of himself and me, playing with Max, rolling over and saying that he couldn't get enough of me.

My chest ached just thinking of what he'd achieved in a short amount of time. He broke through my exterior, he got to my core, and I let him in there. I wanted him there because something in the universe told me it would be okay this time. Both my head and my heart wanted him, but they had been wrong before. Tragically wrong.

I rolled over and looked at the clock. It was after one a.m. He'd been out there for nearly an hour. I crept back to the window and he was leaning against a lamppost, hands stuffed in his pockets.

I sent him a text. *You're so stubborn.*

Told band to go to Boston without me.

What? Why?

Not leaving until we talk.

The sound of a siren approached, the screeching wail getting louder. I watched as Peter turned in the direction of the noise. He covered his ears, lights flashed and a police car zipped down my street, weaving through the few cars in its way. Peter returned to his phone.

Thought you called the cops.

Funny.

I shook my head. There he was, on the sidewalk, now stuck

in New York. He'd let the band go to Boston without him. I sent him another text. *If we talk, what would we talk about?*

Us. Is there anything else?

Two minutes.

I'm miserable.

Two minutes.

I buried my head in my hands and walked away from the window. Looking in the mirror on the wall, I saw the same Katie I saw every day—confident and in control on the outside, scared and insecure on the inside. I never used to let anyone other than Gwen see the inside, but I had let Peter see me. He wasn't scared, he didn't pity or dislike the inside. He liked that part of me. He was falling in love with that girl.

I picked up my phone.

Buzzing you up.

I hurried to the intercom and pressed the button. I opened my apartment door, but the stairwell was silent. *That's weird.* I ran to the window to a sight even worse than Peter and Sasha on the couch.

The sidewalk was deserted. He was gone.

CHAPTER FOURTEEN

I DROPPED to the bed with a thunk, combing my hands through my hair. *I fucked up. I let an amazing guy stand out on the stupid sidewalk while I pulled my neurotic self together, thinking he really would wait for me forever.*

Peter wasn't breaking my heart. I was doing it to myself.

I plucked my phone from the bedside table and dialed his number. Voicemail.

"Hey, it's me," I said, my voice wobbly. "I just looked downstairs and you're gone. I don't know if you can forgive me, but if you can, I would love it if we could talk about this. Tell me where you are and I'll come to see you. I'm sorry. I'm a total asshole. You were right. Call me."

I clutched my phone like it was my only lifeline, my knuckles straining. I could feel the blood draining from my face with every passing minute, leaving my cheeks icy cold. *Please call me back. Please.* Max hopped up on the bed and paced, rubbing his head against my hand. He purred. "I know, buddy. I want him to call back, too."

I couldn't take another second, so I called him again, but before there was a single ring, a knock came at my door. *Crap. Mrs. Gunderson.* She must have heard me manically running around the apartment. She always worried if I was up in the middle of the night.

I stumbled for the door, undid the chain latch and turned the deadbolt. "Mrs. G, I'm sorry if I was being noisy." I opened the door.

"Hi."

My heart froze for an instant, but just as fast, Peter made it chug back to life.

"Mrs. G let me in. She saw me outside after the police car went by."

In slow motion, I took his arm and tugged him inside. Part of me was terrified to make any sudden moves. Like he might disappear. "You didn't leave." I couldn't let go of him. I searched his face, wondering if he was real.

"Of course not. I told you I wouldn't. But I really had to pee. Mrs. G let me use her bathroom. Then she ordered me up here."

I stepped closer, pressing my palm against the side of his face. Stubble poked my hand. His skin was warm, with an indescribable tawny hue to his cheeks. He grinned hesitantly. "You didn't leave."

"Katie, honey, I told you." He took my hand. "I messed up with the only other girl I ever loved. I'm not letting you go unless you tell me you don't love me too."

My pulse steadily thumped in my ears. "The only other girl you loved?"

He smiled and his entire face lit up. "I love you, Katie."

His words lifted a weight. That stupid heart of mine? The one too heavy to carry around anymore? It felt different now. Brand new and perfect. "I love you too, Peter. I'm so sorry." For the first time ever, I felt the past fading away, slipping back where it belonged, as if it was an unwelcome dream I might someday remember only in bits and pieces.

He wrapped his arms around my waist. "You love me?"

I took a deep breath. His warm and woodsy scent was intoxicating, the way I wanted my sheets to smell every morning. Every nerve ending in my body was now raw with anticipation. "I do. I love you so much."

"That's all I needed to hear." He pulled me against him impatiently and my fingers combed into his thick hair. His mouth descended upon mine with a tenderness that only made me want to melt into him.

We kissed as if we were discovering each other, but it was different than that first night in Miami, now that there was love between us. Our lips moved together in perfect sync as he pressed his palms into my lower back, as though he couldn't stand any distance between us at all. He slid his hand to the back of my thigh, raising my leg until it was hitched around his hip. I wrapped my other leg around his waist as he lifted me and motored us to the other side of the room still kissing. Standing before the bed, he carefully lowered me to the mattress. Max was asleep on the pillow.

"Sorry, little man," he said, picking up Max and gently setting him on the floor. "I get her all to myself right now."

He unbuttoned his shirt, his eyes feeding the need burning inside me, the look an ethereal combination of pure, sweet love and unfettered desire. My breath escaped slowly as he rolled his shoulders out of the sleeves while his hair swept across his forehead. I would never, ever, tire of watching him do that.

I arched my back, settling my hips into the bed. Heat blazed in my belly and chest. All I could think about was his hands and lips and every other part of him all over me. I hooked my thumbs beneath the waistband of my silky pajama pants.

"Stop," Peter said. He unbuttoned and unzipped his jeans,

but he never took his eyes from me. "That's my job." He dropped his pants and shed his boxer briefs, my lips quivering with the deep need to please him.

Peter sat on the bed next to me and my head rolled to the side to watch him. He liberated me from my pajama bottoms and cocked an eyebrow when he saw that I wasn't wearing any panties. He stretched out next to me, on his side. His fingers raked lightly up one of my thighs, starting at the knee. I sank into the moment, lost in his eyes, needing our connection. My breath caught up in my throat, leaking out in silent gasps with every inch he traveled closer to the apex between my legs. He stopped short, smiling when I squirmed. He reached across to the other leg, this time exercising inhuman patience as he repeated his glorious torture.

"Touch me," I said. "Please."

"You're so impatient." He sat up and shifted, kneeling between my legs. He slid his hands under my tank top, warm palms flat against my belly. He skimmed my skin, peeling back the garment, cleverly maneuvering around my breasts as he lifted it over my head.

I held my breath as his hands bracketed my ribs and his mouth drifted closer to my chest. The anticipation of his tongue lapping my sensitive skin left my breasts full and warm, my nipples rigid and tight. He opened his mouth and huffed hot air against them. The gentle rush of his breath alone made me feel like I might explode.

"Peter, honey, touch me. I love you. I want you."

He grinned and his eyes flashed with satisfaction. He not only knew how to set an inferno inside me, he knew exactly how to stoke it. "Like this?" He pursed his lips around my nipple. His tongue flicked and rolled against the taut skin. The sensation came as a flood, hot and wet, coursing through my chest, snaking its way the length of my body.

"Yes." My hands followed the contours of his back, along his spine, to the curve of his ass.

He switched to my other breast, slipping his hand between our bellies. My head dropped back when he ventured between my fevered, tender folds. He moaned, exploring the slickness, expertly seeking the apex, and rocking gently with his fingers.

"Oh, God," I muttered. "Like that." I arched my back to be closer to him, reaching between his legs and wrapping my fingers around his cock. He'd been hard before, but it was like trying to squeeze granite. "Kiss me," I whimpered as I pumped his smooth skin. "Please."

He tugged on my nipple with his lips before releasing the suction. His mouth and tongue rode along my jaw, to my chin and back to my ear, where he nipped and nuzzled. "I could spend my whole life with you like this and be happy."

My chest heaved with a weakness for his words. "Kiss me. Please. I need you."

He pecked the corner of my lips, sending a soft sizzle across my mouth. "Good. Because I need you too." His tongue rode delicately along my bottom lip before he ventured inside, our mouths became one, tangling in the heat.

I rubbed his calves and ankles with my feet as we kissed, my hands washing over his back, every molecule of my body starving for him. "Peter, honey, now."

He rolled to my side and reached into the drawer of the bedside table, handing me the foil packet. I opened it as he smiled and stretched out next to me, softly brushing the side of my breast with his fingers. I dipped my head and rolled on the condom, immediately hooking my leg around his hip and muscling him closer. Peter eased me to my back and I welcomed him, kissing him eagerly as he began to stroke inside me.

We rocked in perfect unison, eyes connecting, everything else in the world falling away. I marveled at him, stunning on the inside and out, thinking that if the planets aligned and if I let life happen, we could be blissfully happy together for a very long time. The future, the one I'd feared, was everything I now welcomed. I had him.

He leaned down to kiss away the tear that had rolled down my cheek. "I don't want you to cry. I love you. I want you to be happy."

"I am happy," I said. "More than you'll ever know."

———

Peter and I dozed off after we made love, both of us stirring when the sun began to stream through the windows.

"Morning, beautiful," he said after he'd plucked his glasses from the nightstand.

I rolled closer and nuzzled his chest with my nose. "I love the way you smell in the morning."

He chuckled. "I assumed I smell bad." He scooted closer to me as a comically confused look crossed his face. "Did you forget to shave?"

A lump between us began to move beneath the comforter. "I think somebody's jealous."

Peter ducked under the covers and returned with Max. He stroked his head and rubbed his ears. "I know it's hard, buddy, but we're going to have to learn to share her."

Max wriggled free and stretched before settling in again at the foot of the bed.

I brushed Peter's floppy hair from his forehead. "What time do you have to leave for Boston?"

He cleared his throat and took my hand, playing with each of my fingers. "I need to call the car service and see what they say. Eleven. Noon at the latest is my guess."

I fought the drag at the corners of my mouth, not wanting to think about him leaving. "What day do you want me to fly out to meet you?"

"Excellent question. See, I had all of this extra time last night where I was standing out on the sidewalk with nothing to do, so I finalized everything with the bus company."

"Even when you didn't know if I was going to let you into the apartment?"

"Even when you left me alone on a dirty New York street."

I hid my head in my hands, cringing at my behavior. "I'm so sorry."

"Don't be sorry. It'll be a fun story to tell our grandkids one day." He winked when I spread my fingers to look at him and he peeled my hands from my face. "They can get us the bus I want in Toronto. That show isn't until Wednesday, but you could fly up Tuesday. We have a day off. We can play tourist and stay in a swanky hotel and order room service."

I hummed at the mention of the two of us stealing away, spending hours in a cushy bed, alone. "Sounds incredible."

"Will that give you enough time to get packed?"

"I think so." I popped up on to my elbow. "I guess I probably don't need anything more than jeans and t-shirts, huh?"

"Whatever is most comfortable. Don't pack a lot of bras."

"Ha. Funny."

"You should probably wear one when you meet my parents."

"Your parents?"

"Yeah, at the Chicago shows. It's Boston, Toronto, Detroit, then Chicago," he counted out the cities on his fingers. "Five nights. All sold out. I can introduce you to my old buddies. They'll all be jealous."

What a sunny proposition—making a connection with his past, having him fold me into his life. "I can't wait. I hope your parents like me."

"Are you kidding? They're going to love you."

"What happens after Chicago?"

"Minneapolis, St. Louis, Denver, then out to the West Coast. We finish the middle of September."

"Back to Chicago after that?" I wished I could disguise the anxiousness in my voice, but this was my sole remaining doubt.

He tilted his head and put his finger under my chin, looking at me with sweet but prying eyes. "Are you worried about the Chicago versus New York thing?"

"A little. I'd be lying if I said I don't think about it."

"Come here." He pulled me into his warm embrace and traced his fingers across my back. "You know what? We're lucky to have jobs where we travel all the time. Money isn't an issue for either of us. I figure we just work around our schedules. We can spend time in Chicago, but I'm cool with spending lots of time in New York too."

My heart skipped. "Really?"

"Max and I already discussed it. He's fine with me staying here as long as I don't hog the bed."

I smirked and snuggled closer to him.

"The band is going to take some time off next year. As long as we talk about it and are both willing to make some compromises, I think we can make it work until then. Scratch that. We have to make it work. Phone sex only gets me so far."

"I don't know. You're pretty good at it."

"Uh, correction, I'm good at it with you." Peter pressed his hand against my lower back, urging my hips closer as he nibbled at my ear. "I'd still rather have the real thing."

"Mmm. I like where you're going with this." I hooked my leg around his and stroked the back of his calf with my foot. "Do we have time for the real thing before you have to go?"

"Katie, honey." He dug his fingers into my hair as his tender lips skimmed the base of my throat. "We'll make time."

THE END

———

Thanks so much for reading! If you enjoyed *Rock Starred*, sign up for Karen's newsletter for info on new releases, sales, and exclusive newsletter giveaways. And leave a review online if you can!

It's a huge help.

If you want more from Karen, check out *Bring Me Back*, a dream-come-true series-starter with a British rock star hero and a single mom on the brink of 40. *Secrets of a (Somewhat) Sunny Girl* is a sexy, funny, and heartfelt stand-alone with an Irish rock star hero and a heroine who's super skeptical of love.

ABOUT KAREN BOOTH

Karen Booth is a midwestern girl transplanted in the South, raised on '80s music and too many readings of *Forever* by Judy Blume. An early preoccupation with rock 'n' roll led her to spend her twenties working her way from intern to executive in the music industry. Now she's a married mom of two and instead of staying up late in rock clubs, she gets up before dawn to write sexy contemporary romance and women's fiction.

Karen is co-founder of the 4000+ member Seasoned Romance Facebook group, devoted to the promotion of romance with characters 35+. She has been a finalist for RT Magazine's Series Romance of the Year, RT Magazine's Gold Seal of Excellence, the National Excellence in Romance Fiction Award (NERFA), the Booksellers' Best Award, and the Holt Medallion. Her books have been translated into seventeen languages.

ALSO BY KAREN BOOTH

The Forever series:

Bring Me Back and the sequel, Back Forever

Wishing

Save a Prayer

Claire's Diary

Stand-alone books:

Secrets of a (Somewhat) Sunny Girl

Hiding in the Spotlight

Rock Starred

The KISS Principle

The Eden Empire series:

A Christmas Temptation

A Cinderella Seduction

A Bet with Benefits

A Christmas Rendezvous

The Sterling Wives trilogy:

Once Forbidden, Twice Tempted

High Society Secrets

All He Wants for Christmas

Find more at karenbooth.net